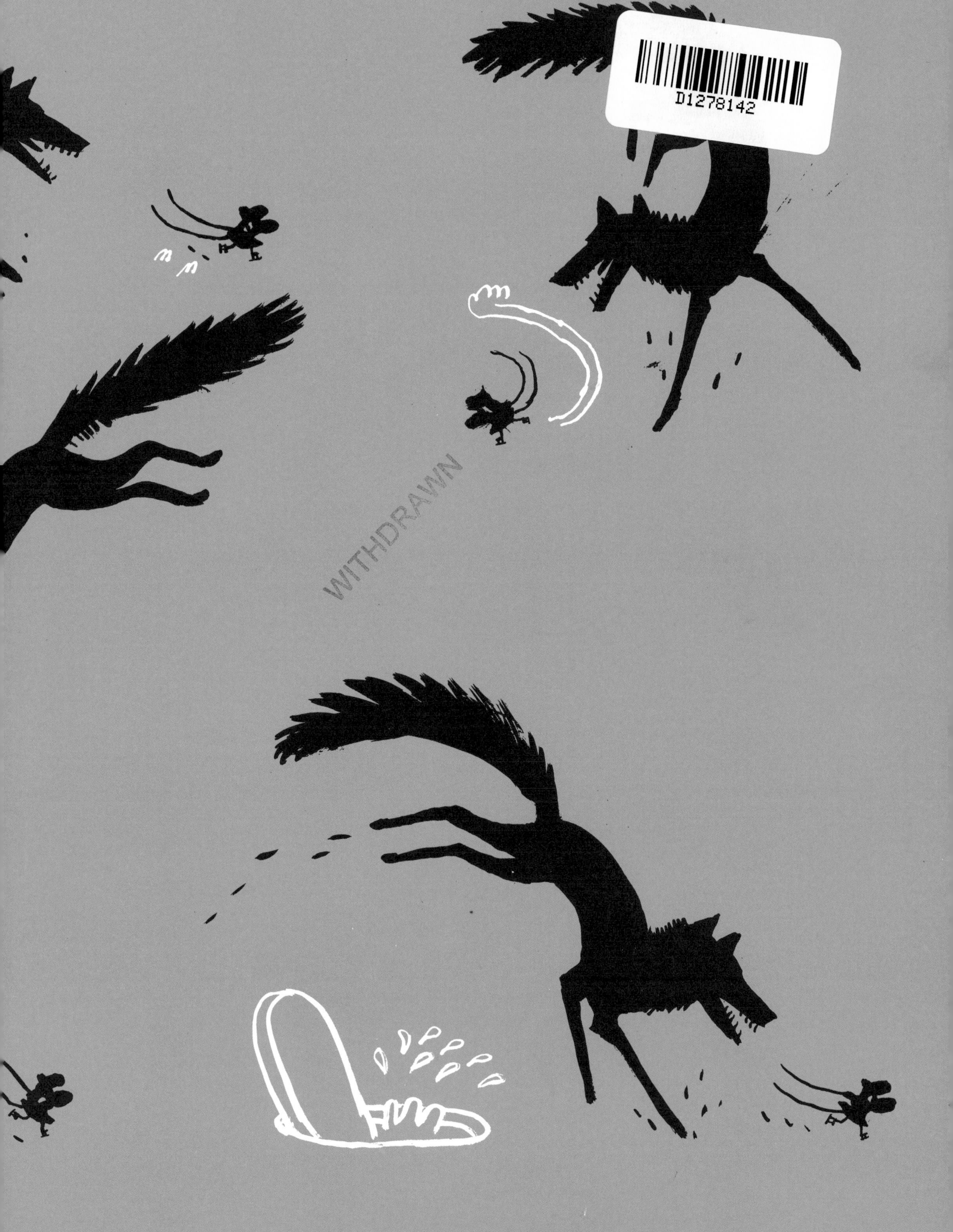

KICKLIY

THE TEARS OF THE PAINTER

BOOKS

PEFC Certified

This product is from sustainably managed forests and controlled sources.

10-31-1800   pefc-france.org

ISBN 978-1-941250-19-8
First Edition, OCTOBER 2017
Printed in France.

DISTRIBUTED TO THE TRADE BY
Consortium Book Sales & Distribution
LLC. 34 Thirteenth Avenue NE
Suite 101, Minneapolis, MN 55413-1007.
cbsd.com, Orders: (800) 283-3572

ododbooks.com

WOOOOOOOOOOOOOVVV

My MASTER was the MEANEST squirrel that I had ever met, but he was BRILLIANT and understood the ARTS like no other.

WOOOOOOOOOOVVVV

Not many APPRENTICES would last under his STRICT teaching conditions.

WOOOOOOVVV

Those who left and tried to paint on their own were BLACKLISTED for life- But me, I chose to stay until the BITTER end.

My Master did not let me touch a BRUSH for TEN WHOLE YEARS,

WAP WAP WAP

Instead, he made me SWEEP his floors, prepare his PAINT, and build his CANVASES—

WAP WAP WAP

What does BLACKLISTED mean, RÉMI?

Well, MUS...

1

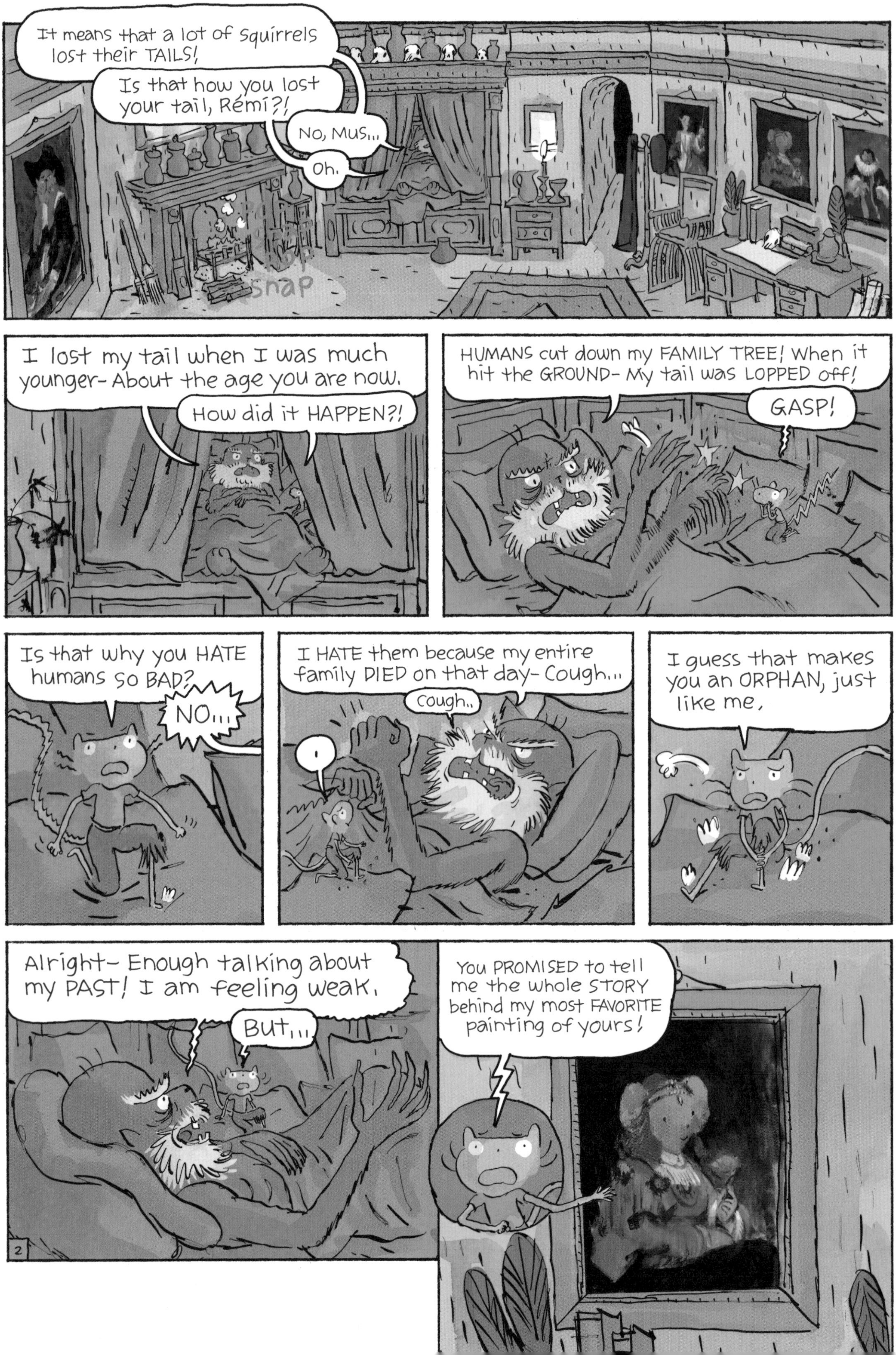

It means that a lot of squirrels lost their TAILS!
Is that how you lost your tail, Rémi?!
No, Mus...
Oh.
snap
I lost my tail when I was much younger- About the age you are now.
How did it HAPPEN?!
HUMANS cut down my FAMILY TREE! When it hit the GROUND- My tail was LOPPED off!
GASP!
Is that why you HATE humans so BAD?
NO...
I HATE them because my entire family DIED on that day- Cough...
Cough..
I guess that makes you an ORPHAN, just like me.
Alright- Enough talking about my PAST! I am feeling weak.
But...
You PROMISED to tell me the whole STORY behind my most FAVORITE painting of yours!

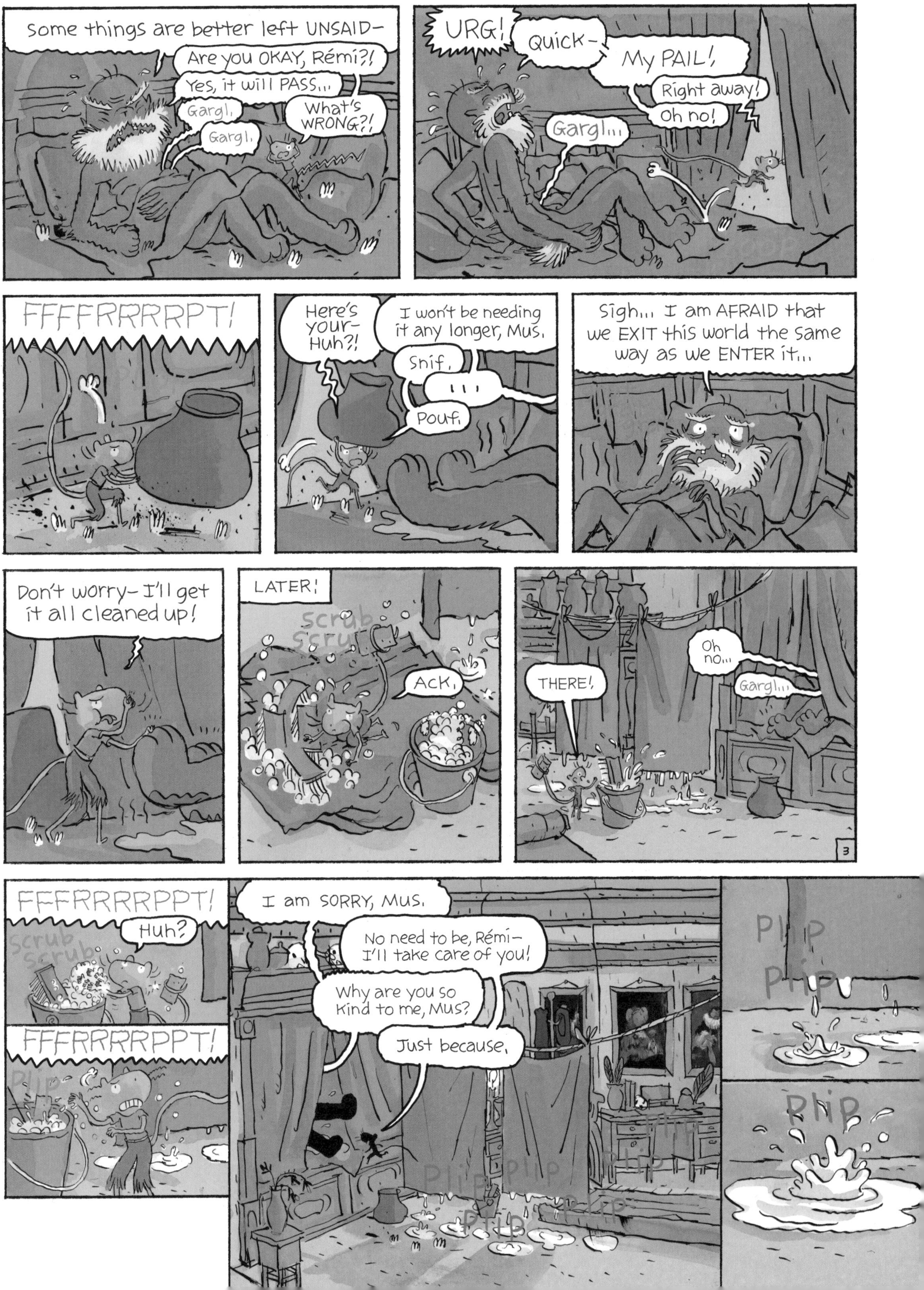
Some things are better left UNSAID–
Are you OKAY, Rémi?!
Yes, it will PASS...
Gargl.
Gargl.
What's WRONG?!
URG!
QUICK–
My PAIL!
Right away!
Oh no!
Gargl...
FFFFRRRRRPT!
Here's your– Huh?!
I won't be needing it any longer, Mus.
Snif.
...
Pouf.
Sigh... I am AFRAID that we EXIT this world the same way as we ENTER it...
Don't worry– I'll get it all cleaned up!
LATER!
scrub scrub
ACK.
THERE!
Oh no...
Gargl...
3
FFFRRRRRPPT!
Huh?
scrub scrub
FFFRRRRRPPT!
Plip
I am SORRY, Mus.
No need to be, Rémi– I'll take care of you!
Why are you so kind to me, Mus?
Just because.
Plip Plip Plip Plip Plip Plip
Plip
Plip
Plip

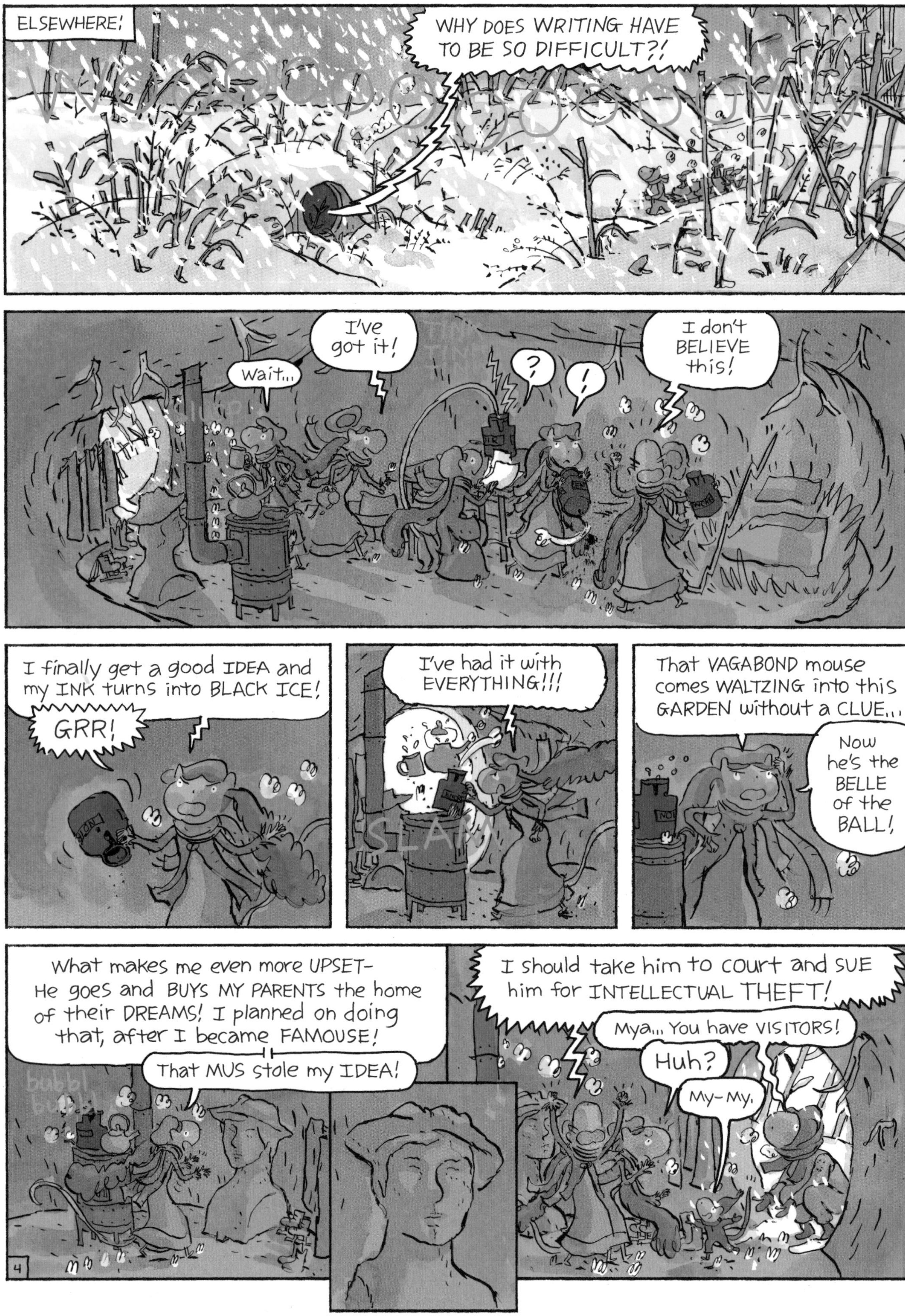
ELSEWHERE!
WHY DOES WRITING HAVE TO BE SO DIFFICULT?!
Wait...
I've got it!
TINK TINK TINK
?
!
I don't BELIEVE this!
I finally get a good IDEA and my INK turns into BLACK ICE!
GRR!
I've had it with EVERYTHING!!!
SLAM
That VAGABOND mouse comes WALTZING into this GARDEN without a CLUE...
Now he's the BELLE of the BALL!
What makes me even more UPSET- He goes and BUYS MY PARENTS the home of their DREAMS! I planned on doing that, after I became FAMOUSE!
That MUS stole my IDEA!
bubbl bubbl
I should take him to court and SUE him for INTELLECTUAL THEFT!
Mya... You have VISITORS!
Huh?
My-My,

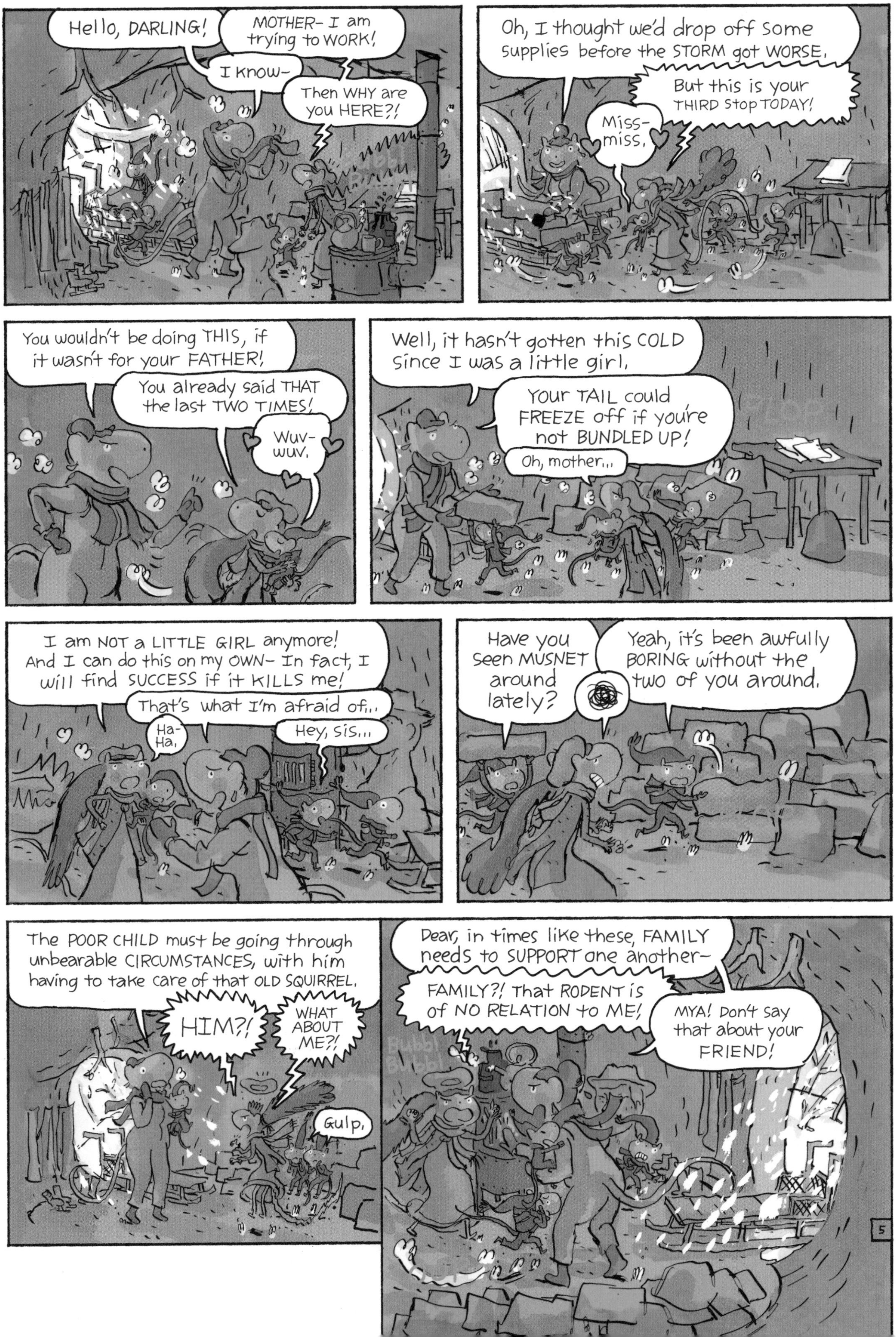
Hello, DARLING!
MOTHER- I am trying to WORK!
I know-
Then WHY are you HERE?!
Oh, I thought we'd drop off some supplies before the STORM got WORSE.
Miss-miss.
But this is your THIRD stop TODAY!
You wouldn't be doing THIS, if it wasn't for your FATHER!
You already said THAT the last TWO TIMES!
Wuv-wuv.
Well, it hasn't gotten this COLD since I was a little girl.
Your TAIL could FREEZE off if you're not BUNDLED UP!
Oh, mother...
I am NOT a LITTLE GIRL anymore! And I can do this on my OWN- In fact, I will find SUCCESS if it KILLS me!
That's what I'm afraid of...
Ha-Ha.
Hey, sis...
Have you seen MUSNET around lately?
Yeah, it's been awfully BORING without the two of you around.
The POOR CHILD must be going through unbearable CIRCUMSTANCES, with him having to take care of that OLD SQUIRREL.
HIM?!
WHAT ABOUT ME?!
Gulp.
Dear, in times like these, FAMILY needs to SUPPORT one another-
FAMILY?! That RODENT is of NO RELATION to ME!
MYA! Don't say that about your FRIEND!

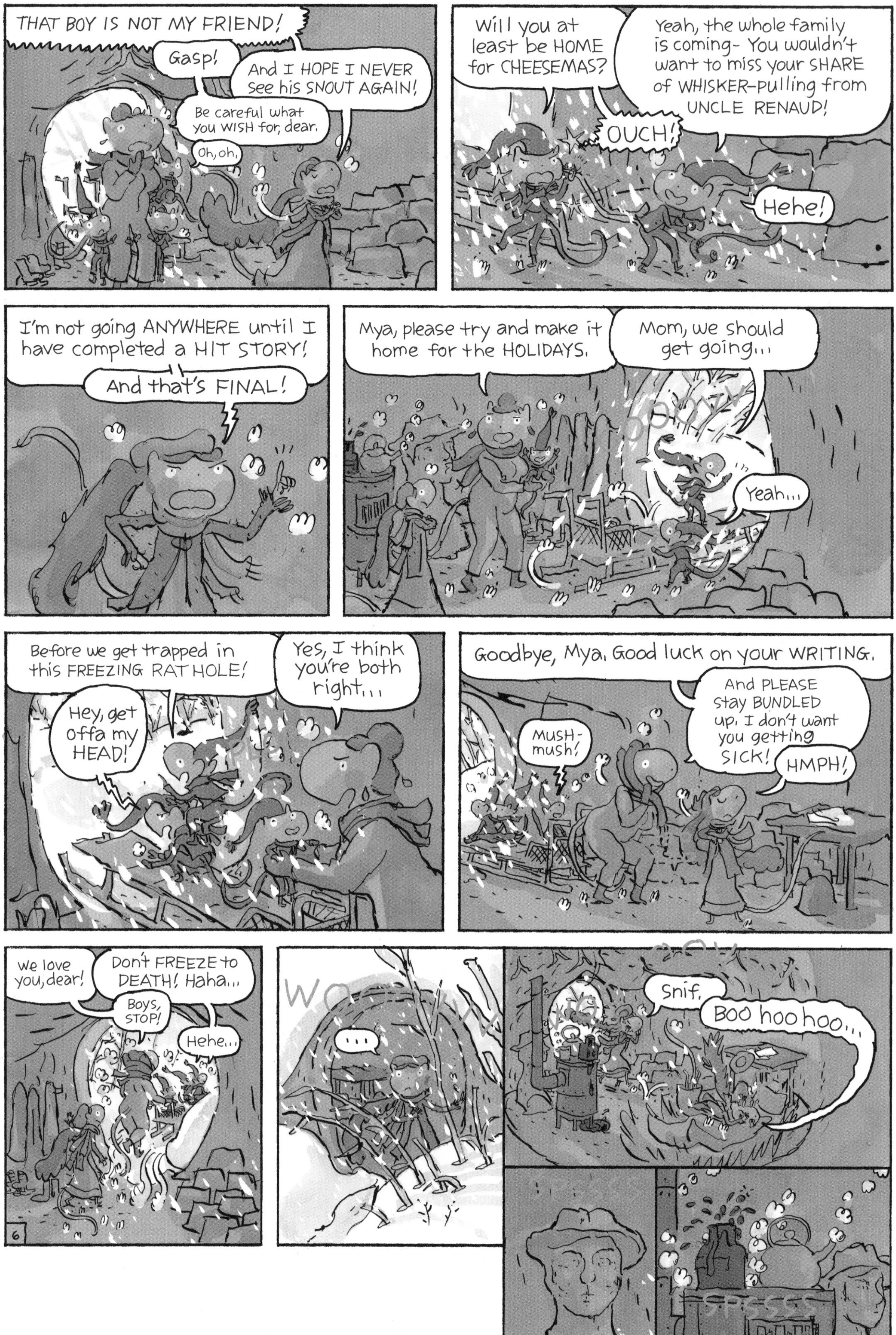
THAT BOY IS NOT MY FRIEND!
Gasp!
And I HOPE I NEVER see his SNOUT AGAIN!
Be careful what you WISH for, dear.
Oh, oh,
Will you at least be HOME for CHEESEMAS?
Yeah, the whole family is coming- You wouldn't want to miss your SHARE of WHISKER-pulling from UNCLE RENAUD!
OUCH!
Hehe!
I'm not going ANYWHERE until I have completed a HIT STORY!
And that's FINAL!
Mya, please try and make it home for the HOLIDAYS.
Mom, we should get going...
Yeah...
Before we get trapped in this FREEZING RAT HOLE!
Yes, I think you're both right...
Hey, get offa my HEAD!
Goodbye, Mya. Good luck on your WRITING.
And PLEASE stay BUNDLED up. I don't want you getting SICK!
MUSH-mush!
HMPH!
We love you, dear!
Don't FREEZE to DEATH! Haha...
Boys, STOP!
Hehe...
...
Snif.
Boo hoo hoo...
SPSSSS
SPSSSS

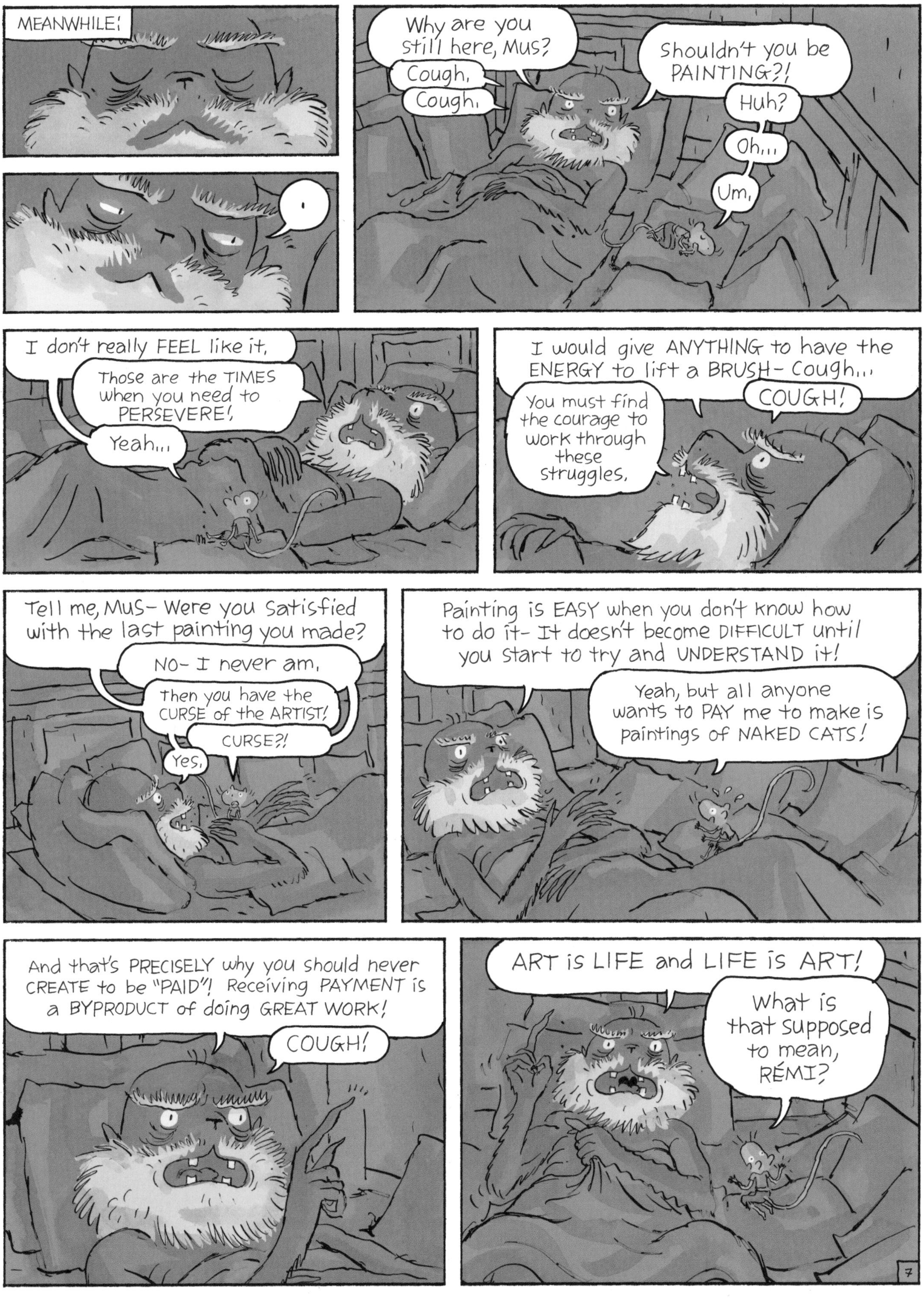
MEANWHILE:
Why are you still here, MUS?
Cough.
Cough.
Shouldn't you be PAINTING?!
Huh?
Oh...
Um.
I don't really FEEL like it.
Those are the TIMES when you need to PERSEVERE!
Yeah...
I would give ANYTHING to have the ENERGY to lift a BRUSH- Cough...
COUGH!
You must find the courage to work through these struggles.
Tell me, MUS- Were you satisfied with the last painting you made?
NO- I never am.
Then you have the CURSE of the ARTIST!
CURSE?!
Yes.
Painting is EASY when you don't know how to do it- It doesn't become DIFFICULT until you start to try and UNDERSTAND it!
Yeah, but all anyone wants to PAY me to make is paintings of NAKED CATS!
And that's PRECISELY why you should never CREATE to be "PAID"! Receiving PAYMENT is a BYPRODUCT of doing GREAT WORK!
COUGH!
ART is LIFE and LIFE is ART!
What is that supposed to mean, RÉMI?

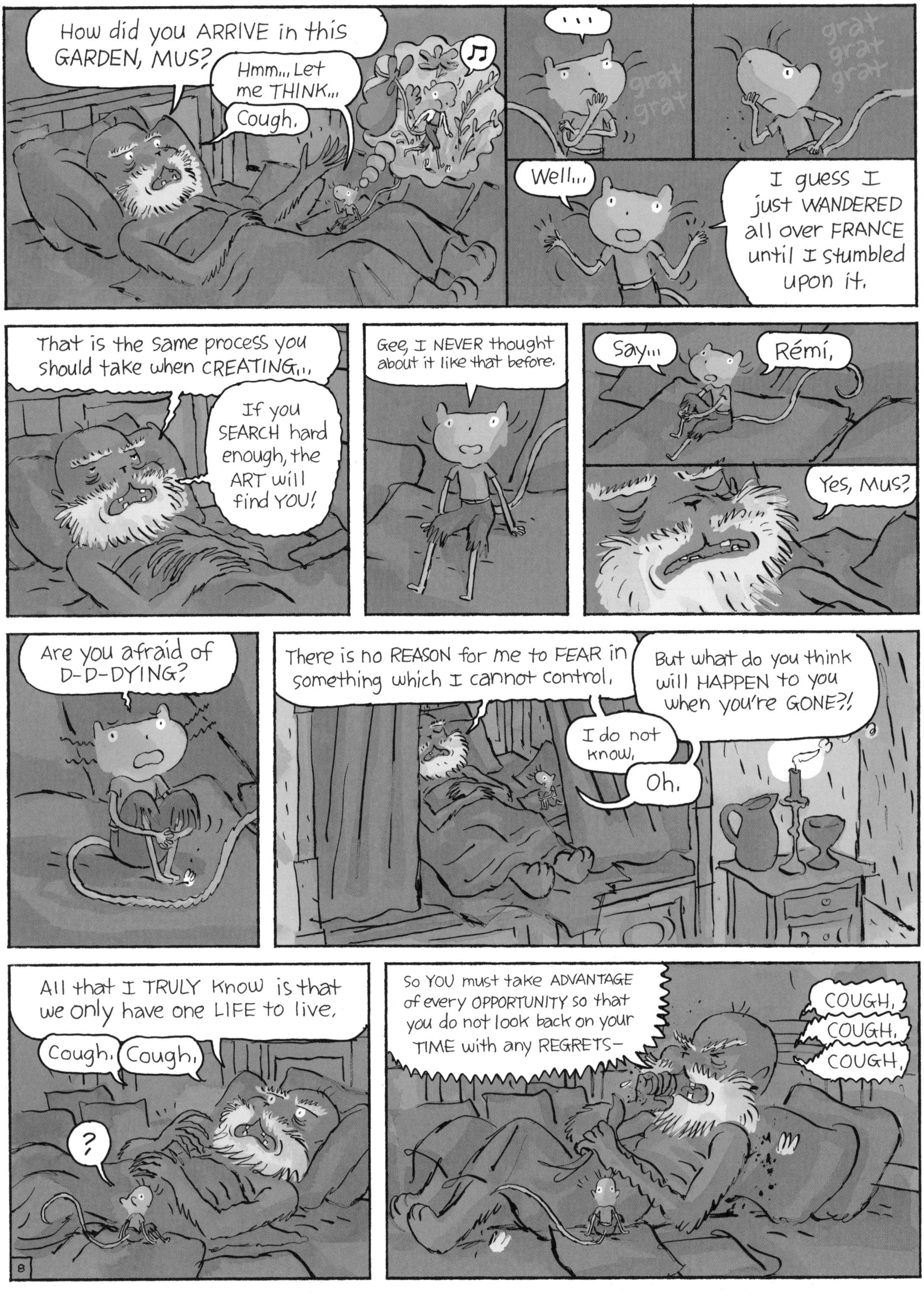
How did you ARRIVE in this GARDEN, MUS?
Hmm... Let me THINK...
Cough.
...
grat grat
grat grat grat
Well...
I guess I just WANDERED all over FRANCE until I stumbled upon it.
That is the same process you should take when CREATING...
If you SEARCH hard enough, the ART will find YOU!
Gee, I NEVER thought about it like that before.
Say...
Rémi.
Yes, Mus?
Are you afraid of D-D-DYING?
There is no REASON for me to FEAR in something which I cannot control.
But what do you think will HAPPEN to you when you're GONE?!
I do not know.
Oh.
All that I TRULY know is that we only have one LIFE to live.
Cough. Cough.
?
So YOU must take ADVANTAGE of every OPPORTUNITY so that you do not look back on your TIME with any REGRETS—
COUGH.
COUGH.
COUGH.

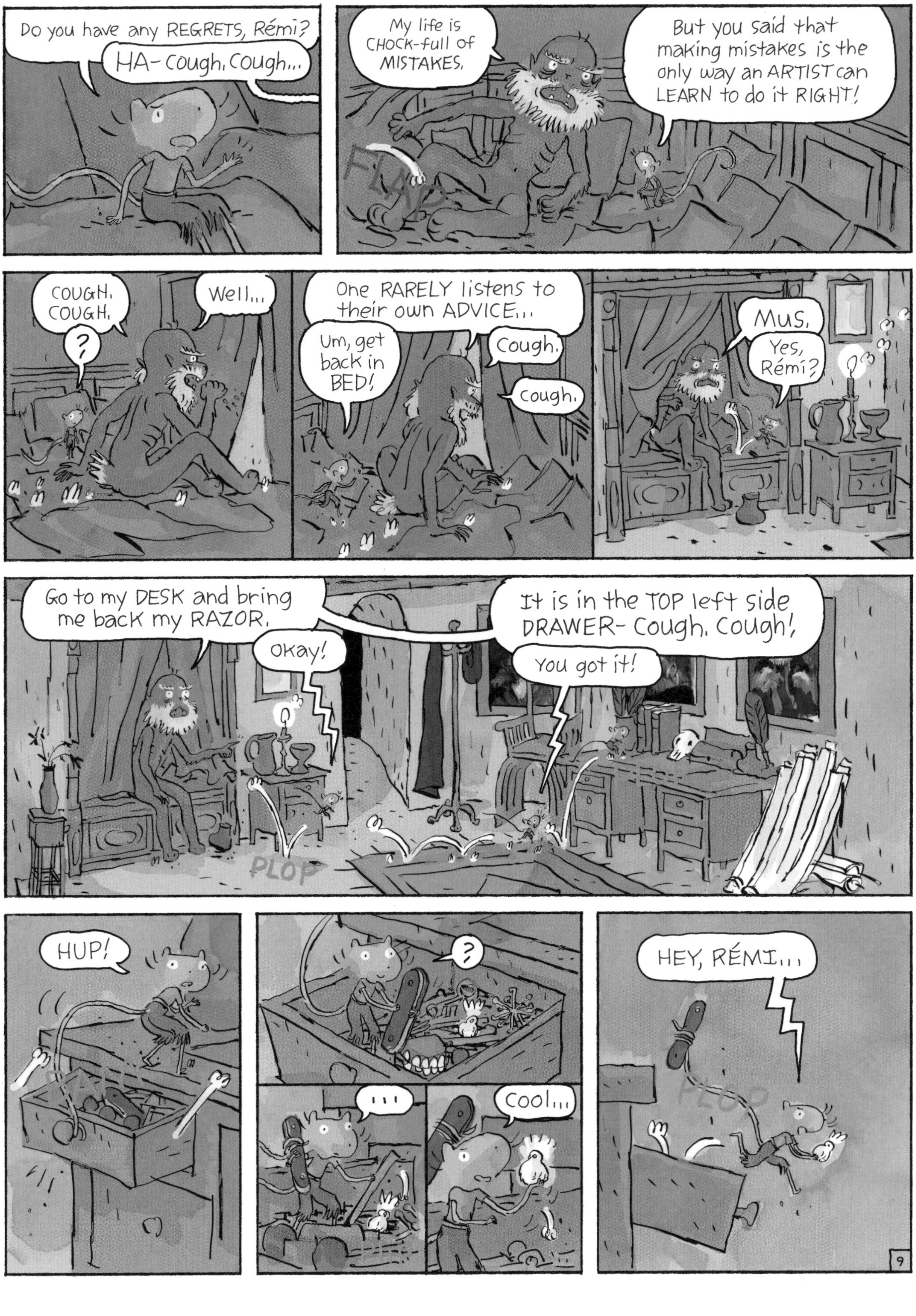
Do you have any REGRETS, Rémi?
HA-cough. Cough...
My life is CHOCK-full of MISTAKES.
But you said that making mistakes is the only way an ARTIST can LEARN to do it RIGHT!
FLAP
COUGH. COUGH.
?
Well...
One RARELY listens to their own ADVICE...
Um, get back in BED!
Cough.
cough.
Mus.
Yes, Rémi?
Go to my DESK and bring me back my RAZOR.
Okay!
It is in the TOP left side DRAWER- Cough. Cough!
You got it!
PLOP
HUP!
?
...
Cool...
HEY, RÉMI...
PLOP

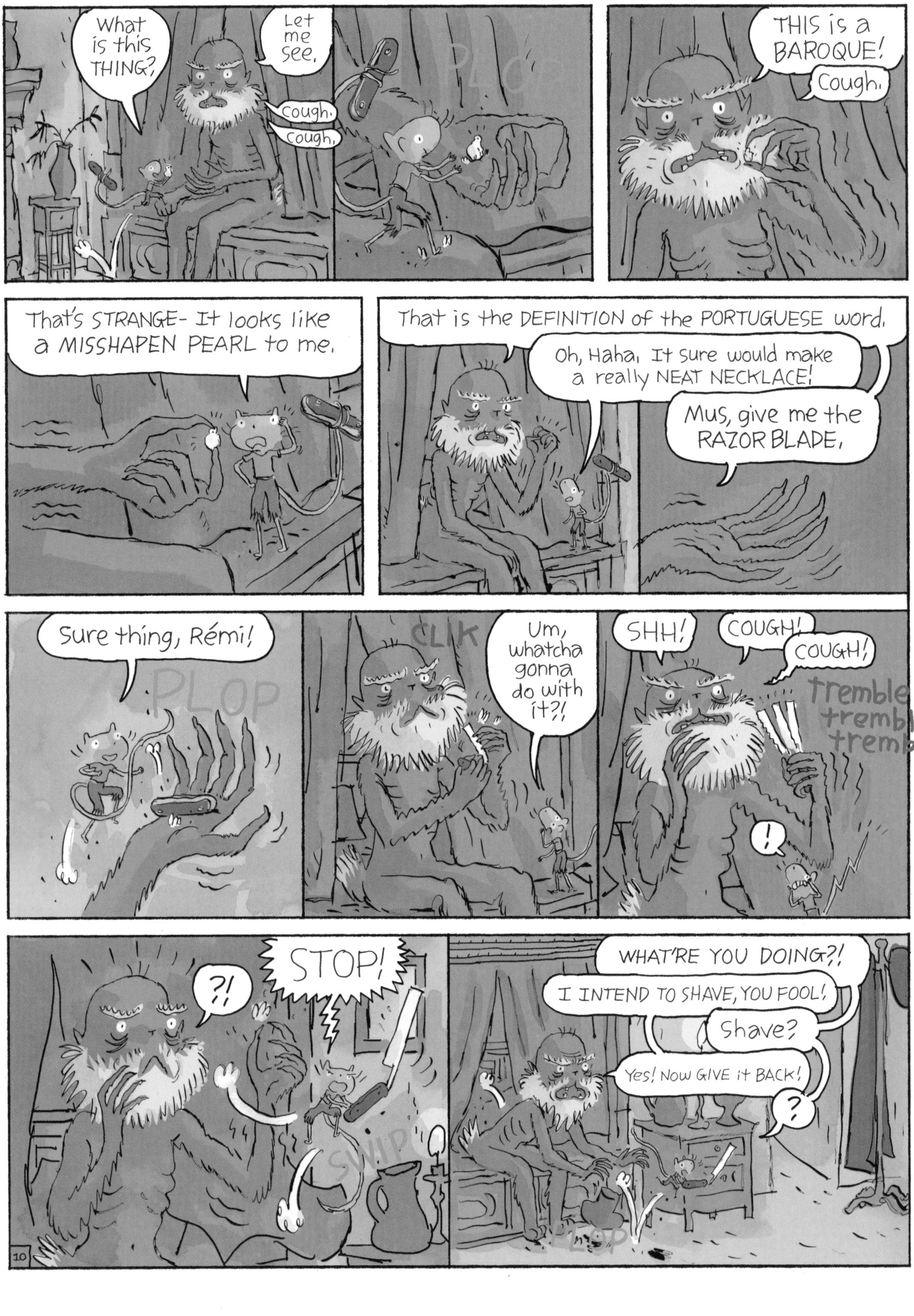
What is this THING?
Let me see.
cough.
cough.
PLOP
THIS is a BAROQUE!
Cough.
That's STRANGE- It looks like a MISSHAPEN PEARL to me.
That is the DEFINITION of the PORTUGUESE word.
Oh, Haha. It sure would make a really NEAT NECKLACE!
Mus, give me the RAZOR BLADE.
Sure thing, Rémi!
PLOP
CLIK
Um, whatcha gonna do with it?!
SHH!
COUGH!
COUGH!
tremble tremble tremble
!
?!
STOP!
SWIP
WHAT'RE YOU DOING?!
I INTEND TO SHAVE, YOU FOOL!
Shave?
Yes! Now GIVE it BACK!
?
PLOP

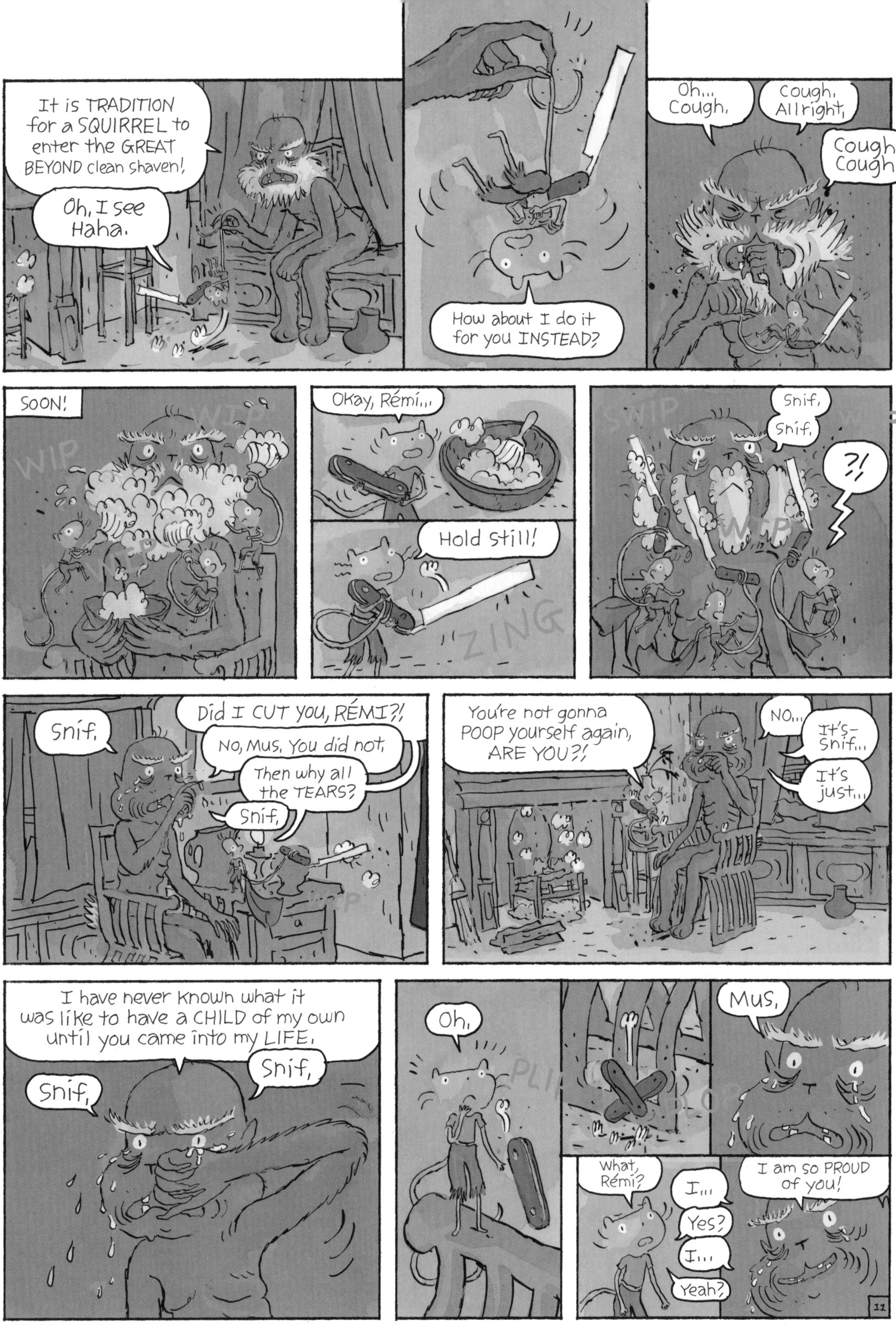
It is TRADITION for a SQUIRREL to enter the GREAT BEYOND clean shaven!
Oh, I see Haha.
How about I do it for you INSTEAD?
Oh... Cough.
Cough. Allright.
Cough. Cough.
SOON!
WIP
WIP
Okay, Rémi...
Hold still!
ZING
SWIP
Snif.
Snif.
?!
WIP
Snif.
Did I CUT you, RÉMI?!
No, Mus. You did not.
Then why all the TEARS?
Snif.
You're not gonna POOP yourself again, ARE YOU?!
NO...
It's- Snif...
It's just...
I have never known what it was like to have a CHILD of my own until you came into my LIFE.
Snif.
Snif.
Oh.
Mus.
What, Rémi?
I...
Yes?
I...
Yeah?
I am so PROUD of you!

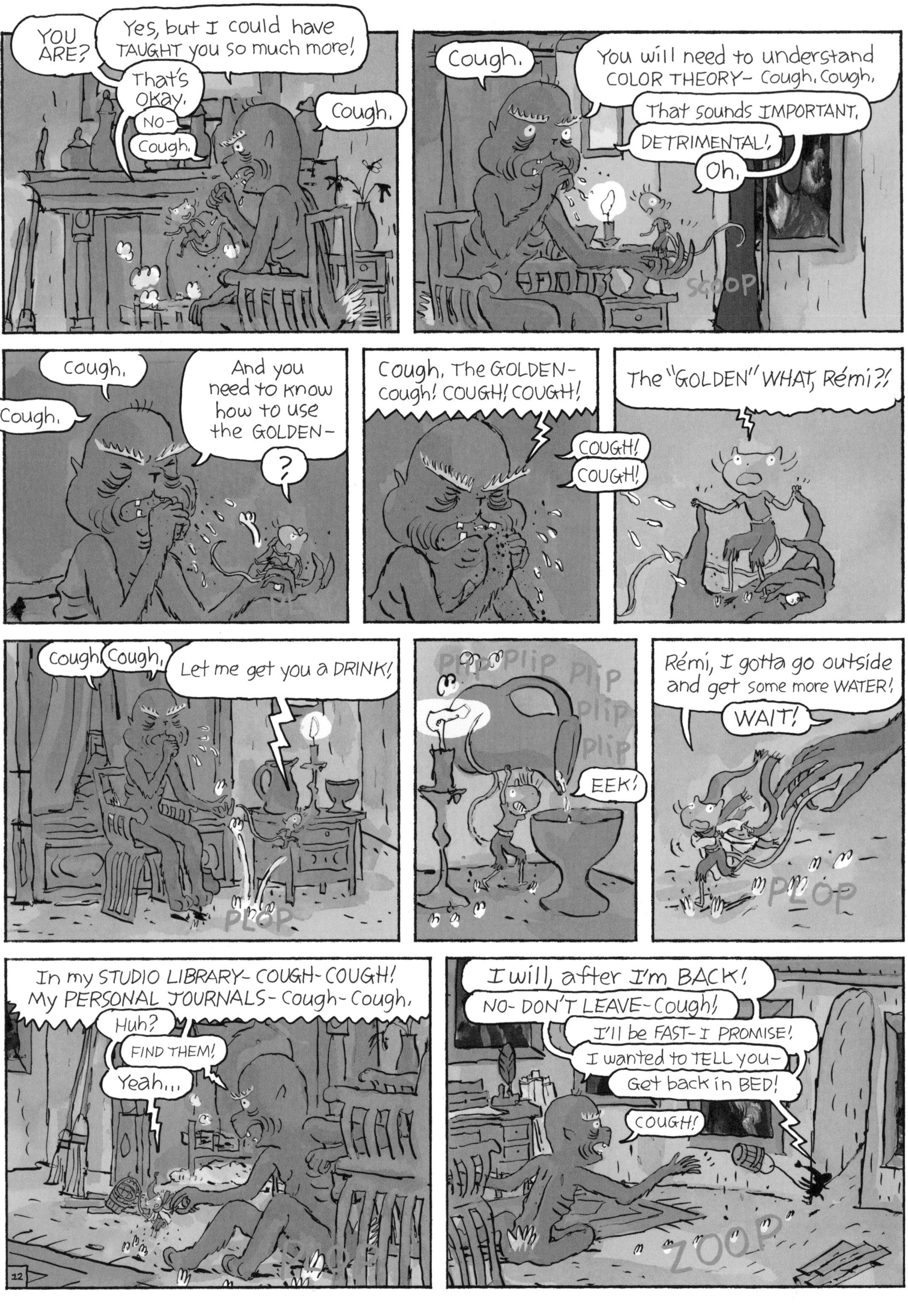
YOU ARE?
Yes, but I could have TAUGHT you so much more!
That's okay.
No-
Cough.
Cough.
Cough.
You will need to understand COLOR THEORY- Cough. Cough.
That sounds IMPORTANT.
DETRIMENTAL!
Oh.
SCOOP
Cough.
Cough.
And you need to know how to use the GOLDEN-
?
PLIP
Cough. The GOLDEN- cough! COUGH! COUGH!
COUGH!
COUGH!
The "GOLDEN" WHAT, Rémi?!
Cough.
Cough.
Let me get you a DRINK!
PLOP
PLIP PLIP PLIP
Plip
Plip
EEK!
Rémi, I gotta go outside and get some more WATER!
WAIT!
PLOP
In my STUDIO LIBRARY- COUGH- COUGH! My PERSONAL JOURNALS- Cough- Cough.
Huh?
FIND THEM!
Yeah...
I will, after I'm BACK!
NO- DON'T LEAVE- Cough!
I'll be FAST- I PROMISE!
I wanted to TELL you-
Get back in BED!
COUGH!
ZOOP

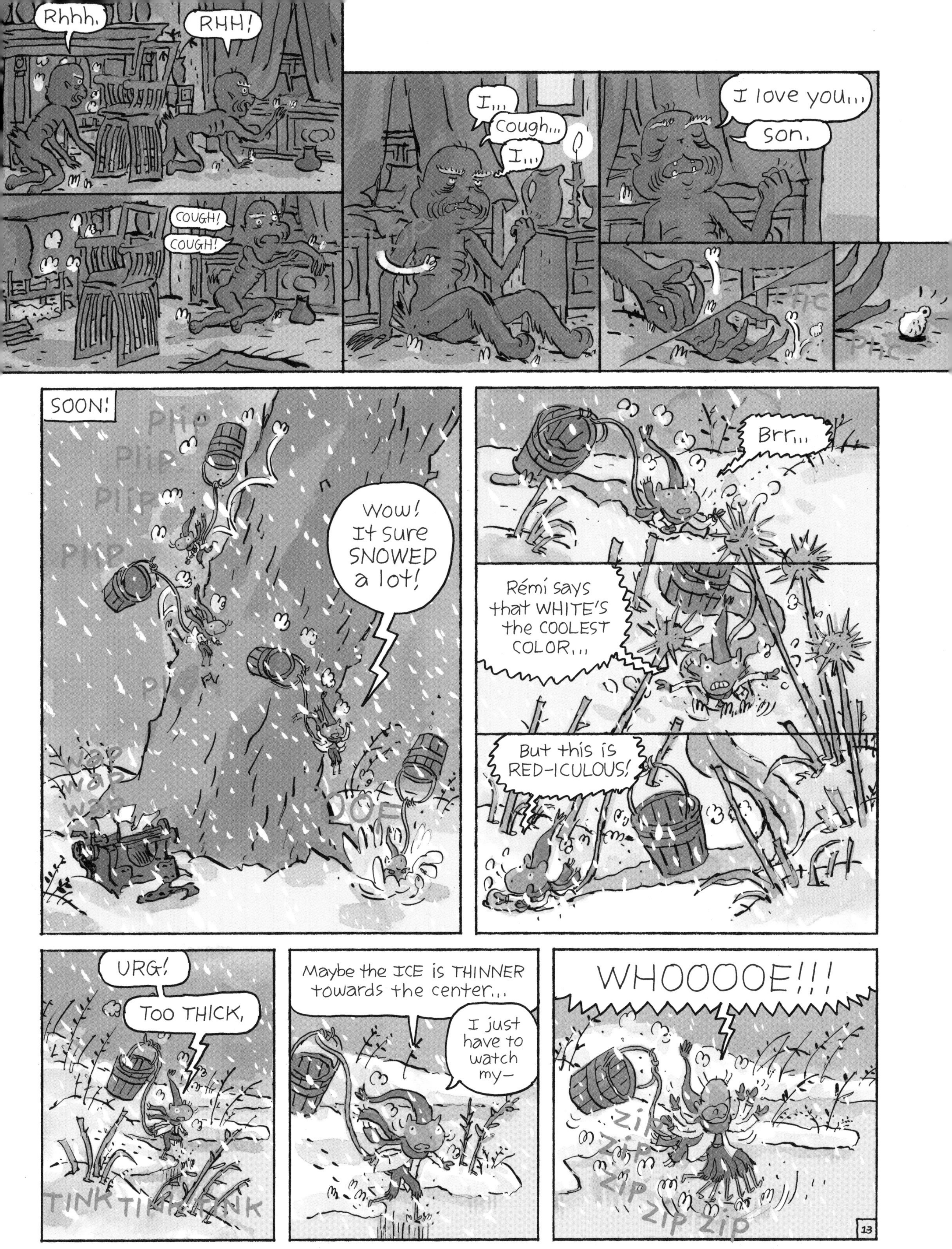

Rhhh.
RHH!
COUGH!
COUGH!
I...
cough...
I...
I love you...
son.
Phc
Phc
SOON!
Plip
Plip
Plip
PLIP
Plip
Wow! It sure SNOWED a lot!
wap
wap
wap
POOF
Brr...
Rémi says that WHITE'S the COOLEST COLOR...
But this is RED-ICULOUS!
URG!
TOO THICK.
TINK TINK TINK
Maybe the ICE is THINNER towards the center...
I just have to watch my-
WHOOOOE!!!
zip
zip
zip
zip
zip

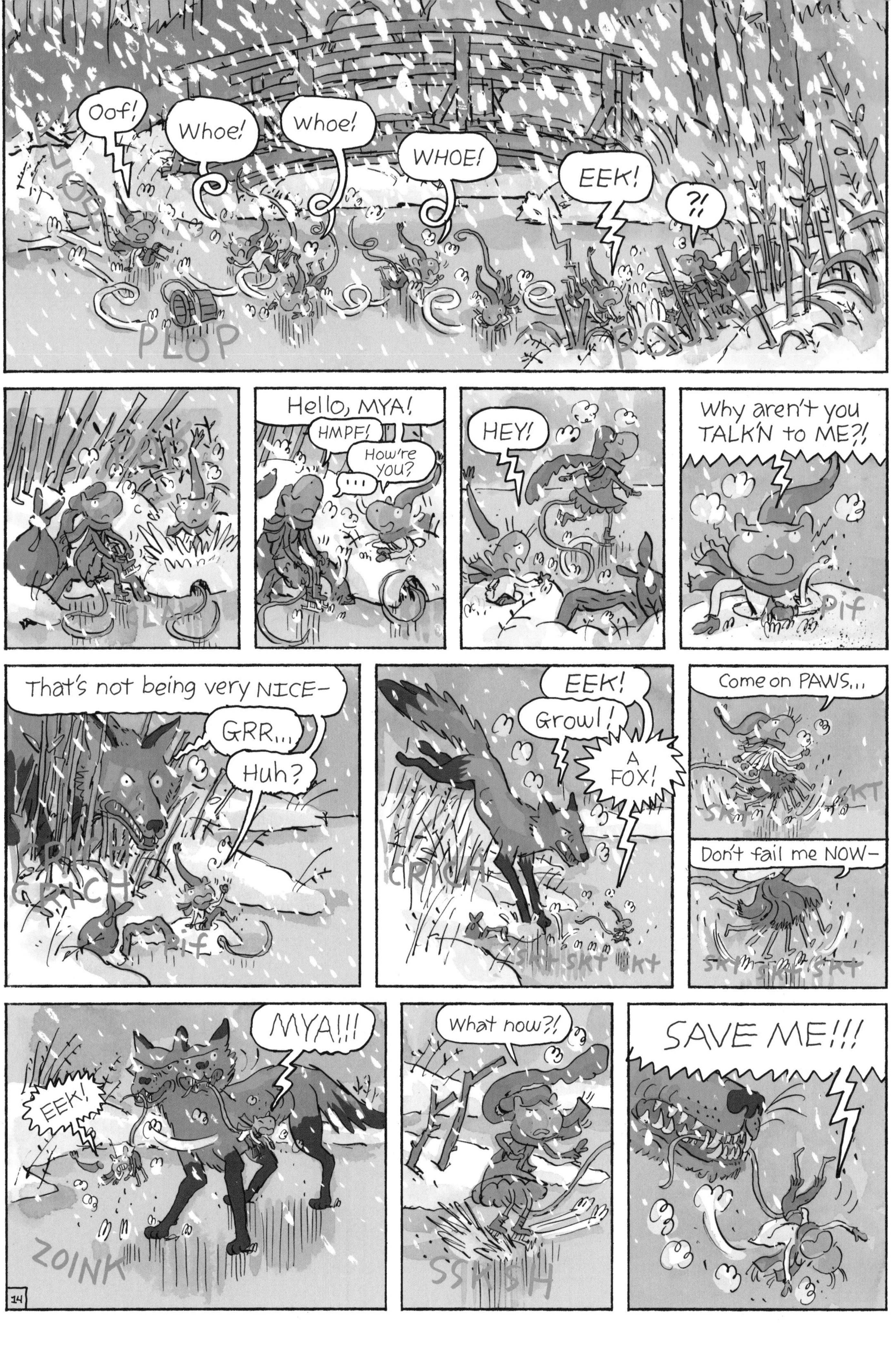
Oof!
Whoe!
whoe!
WHOE!
EEK!
?!
PLOP
Hello, MYA!
HMPF!
How're you?
...
HEY!
Why aren't you TALK'N to ME?!
Pif
That's not being very NICE–
GRR...
Huh?
CRICH
Pif
EEK!
Growl!
A FOX!
CRICH
SKT SKT SKT
Come on PAWS...
SKT SKT
Don't fail me NOW–
SKT SKT SKT
MYA!!!
EEK!
ZOINK
What now?!
SSHISH
SAVE ME!!!

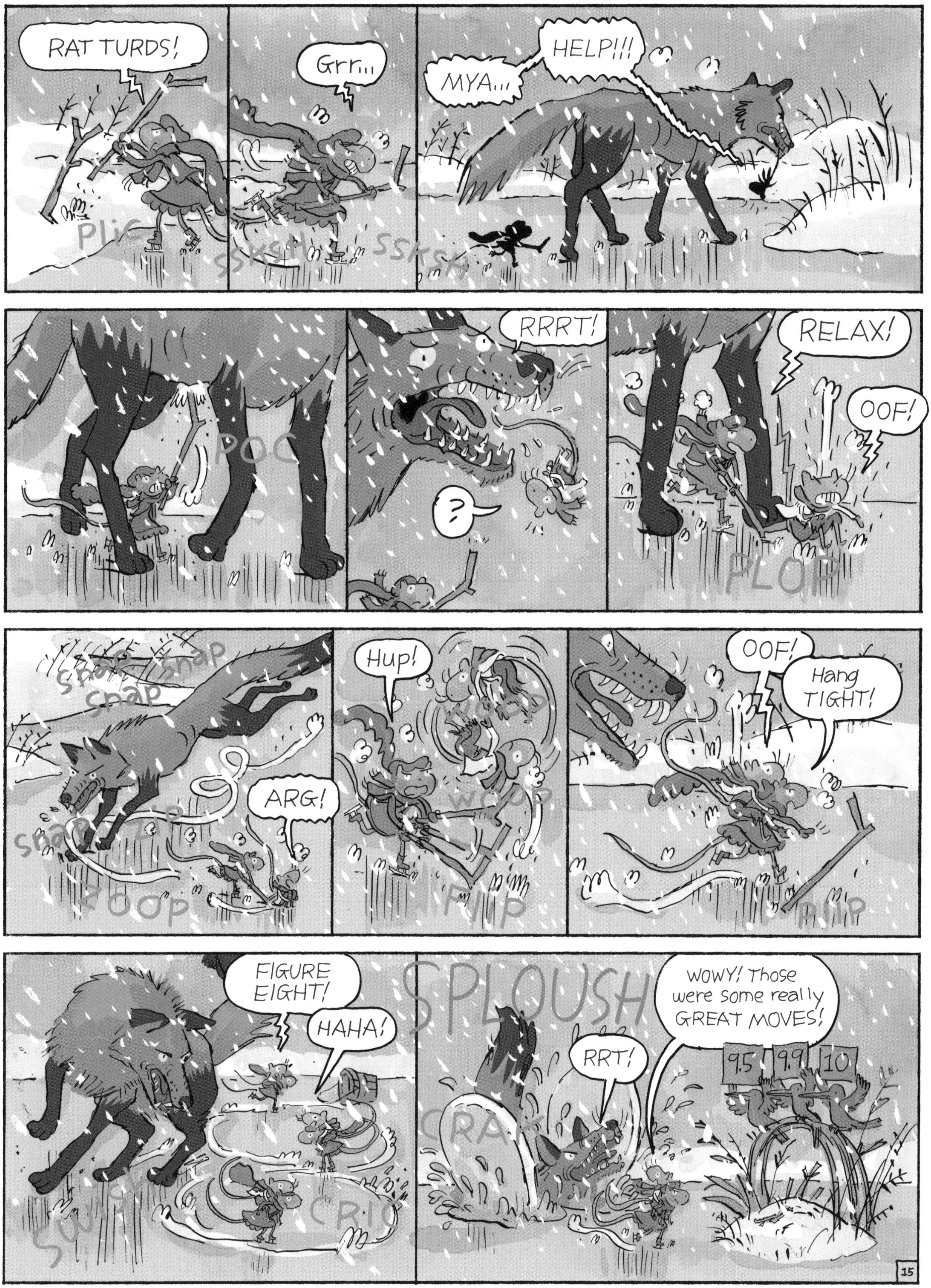

RAT TURDS!
PLIC
Grr...
SSKSH
SSKSH
MYA...
HELP!!!
POC
RRRT!
?
RELAX!
OOF!
PLOP
snap snap
snap
snap
ARG!
ZOOP
Hup!
WOOP
WOOP
FLIP
OOF!
Hang TIGHT!
FLIP
FIGURE EIGHT!
HAHA!
CRIC
SPLOUSH
WOWY! Those were some really GREAT MOVES!
RRT!
9.5
9.9
10
CRAK

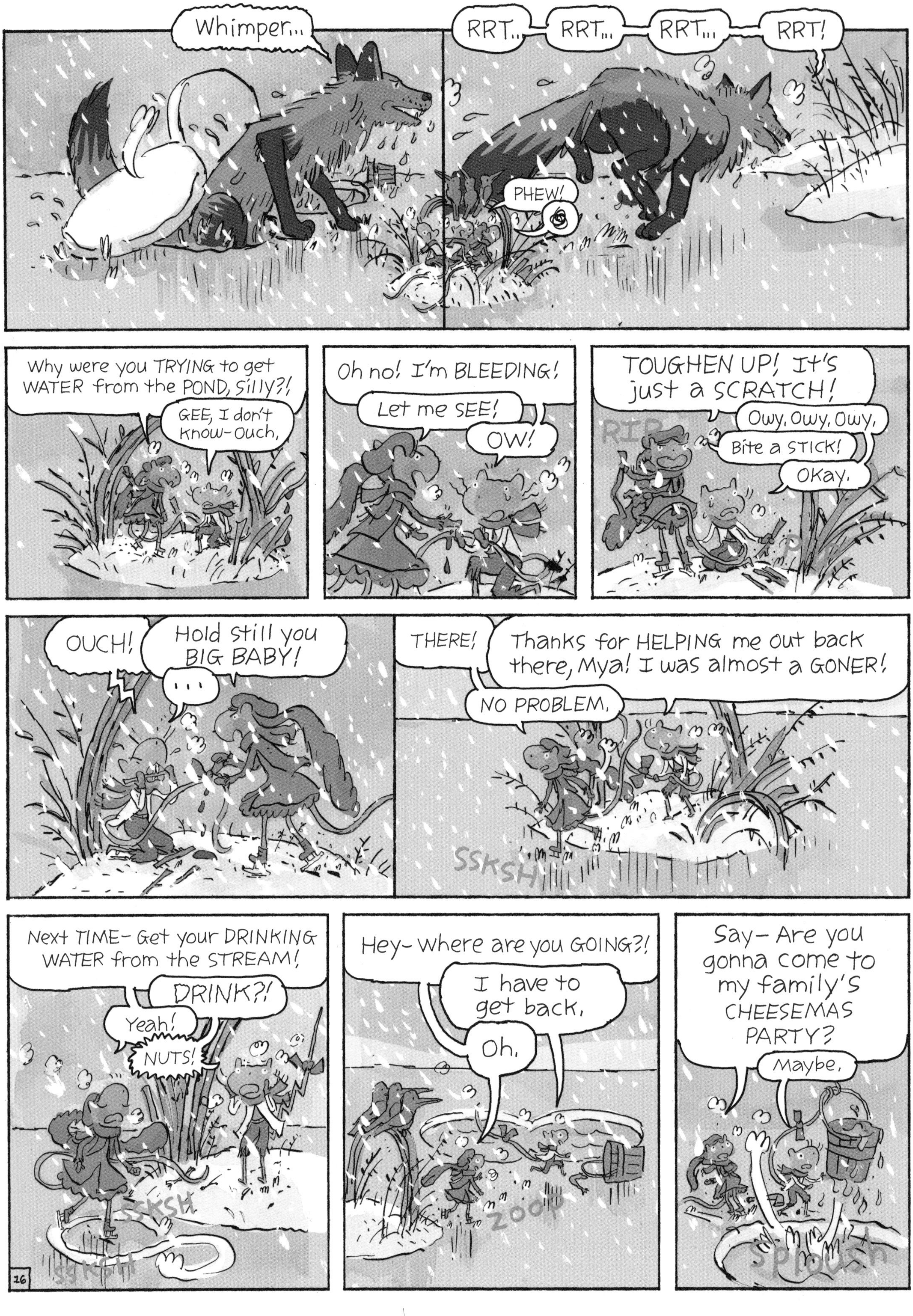

Whimper...
RRT... RRT... RRT... RRT!
PHEW!
Why were you TRYING to get WATER from the POND, silly?!
GEE, I don't know-Ouch.
Oh no! I'm BLEEDING!
Let me SEE!
OW!
TOUGHEN UP! It's just a SCRATCH!
RIP
Owy, Owy, Owy.
Bite a STICK!
OKay.
OUCH!
Hold still you BIG BABY!
...
THERE!
Thanks for HELPING me out back there, Mya! I was almost a GONER!
NO PROBLEM.
SSKSH
Next TIME- Get your DRINKING WATER from the STREAM!
DRINK?!
Yeah!
NUTS!
SSKSH
SSKSH
Hey- Where are you GOING?!
I have to get back.
Oh.
ZOOP
Say- Are you gonna come to my family's CHEESEMAS PARTY?
Maybe.
SPLOOSH

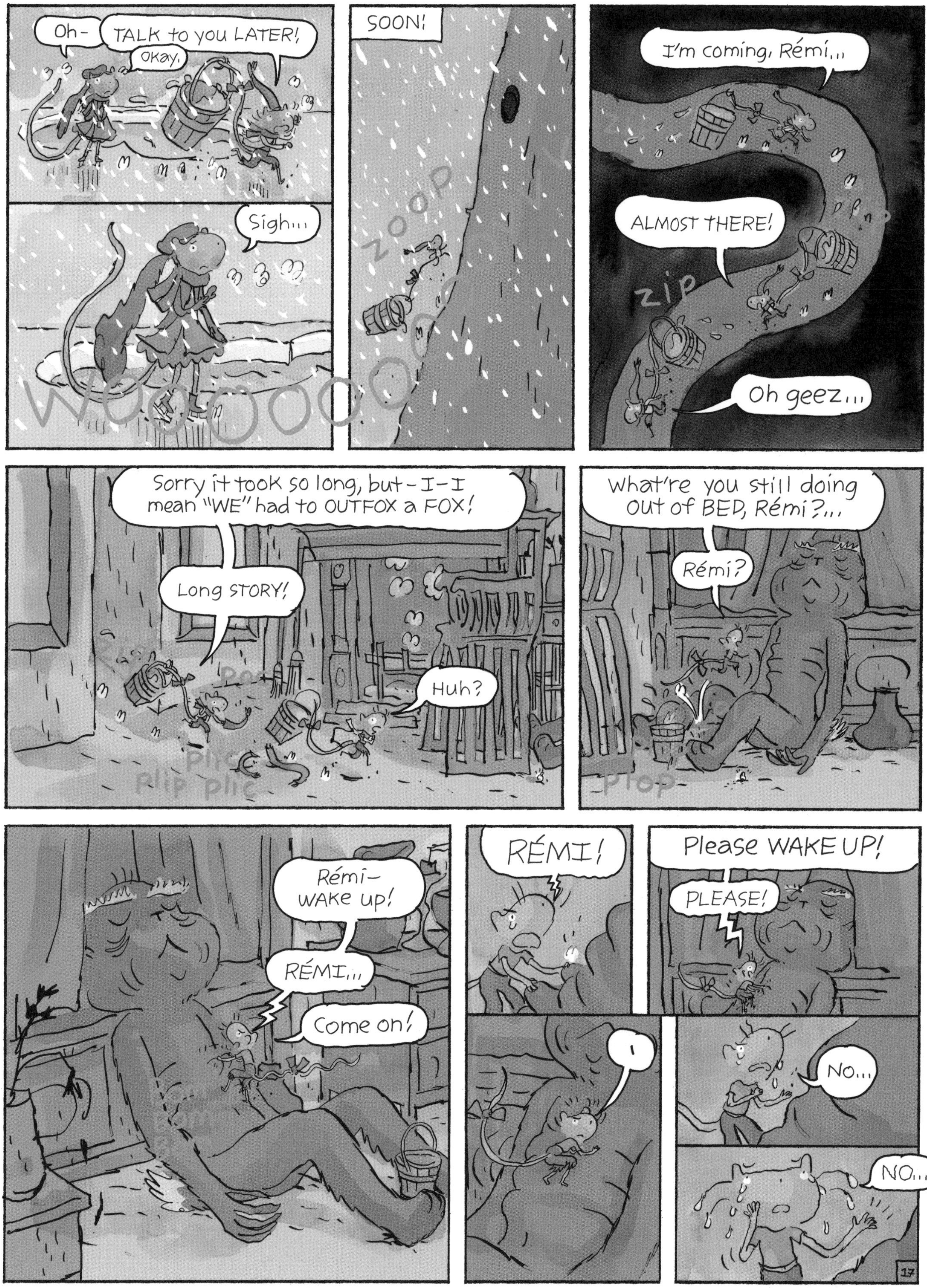
Oh-
TALK to you LATER!
Okay.
Sigh...
WOOOOOOOO
SOON!
ZOOP
I'm coming, Rémi...
ALMOST THERE!
zip
Oh geez...
Sorry it took so long, but-I-I mean "WE" had to OUTFOX a FOX!
Long STORY!
Huh?
Plip plic
Plic
What're you still doing out of BED, Rémi?...
Rémi?
Plop
Rémi-WAKE up!
RÉMI...
Come on!
RÉMI!
Please WAKE UP!
PLEASE!
!
NO...
NO...

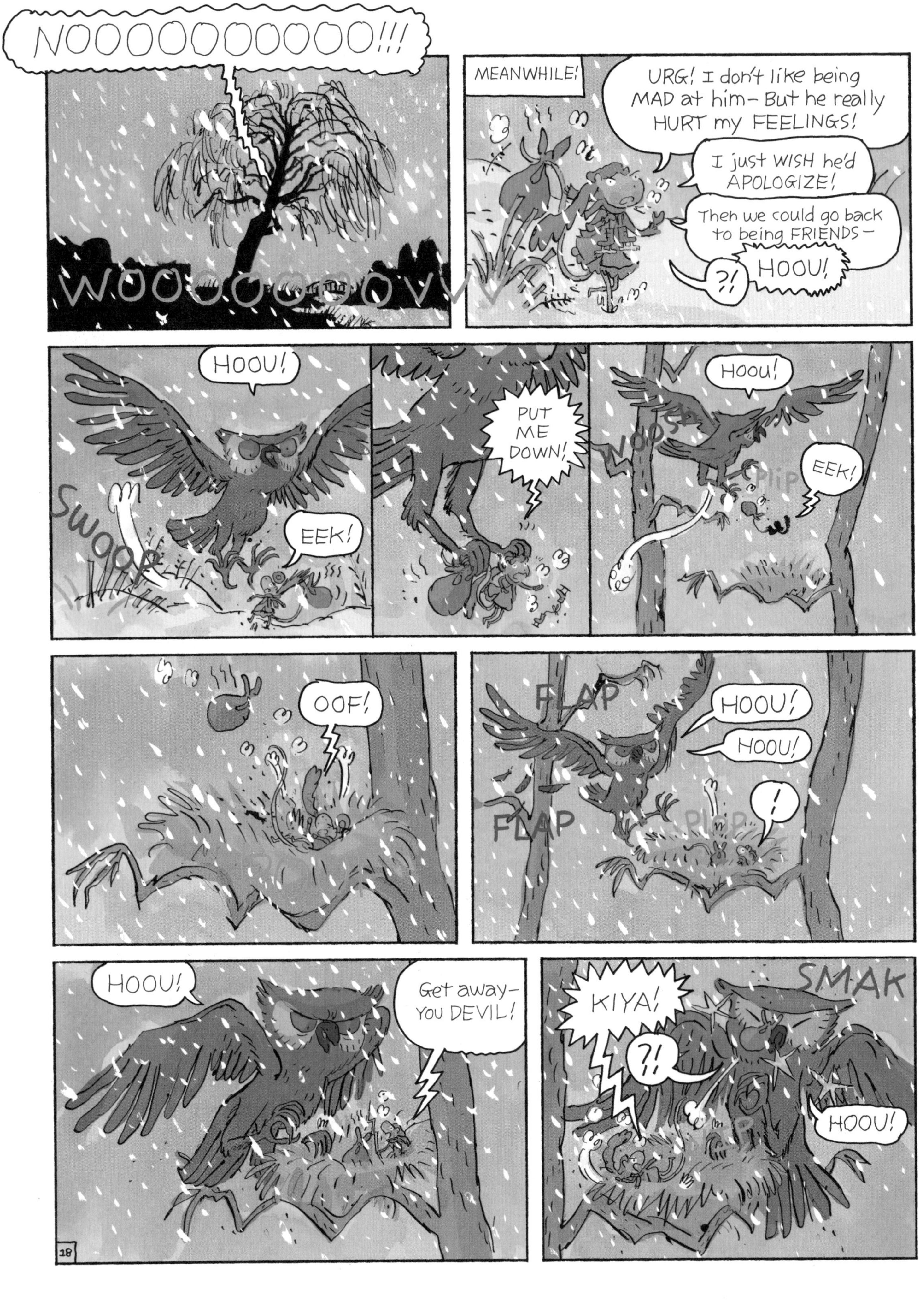

NOOOOOOOOOO!!!
WOOOOOOOOVVV
MEANWHILE!
URG! I don't like being MAD at him- But he really HURT my FEELINGS!
I just WISH he'd APOLOGIZE!
Then we could go back to being FRIENDS-
HOOU!
?!
HOOU!
SWOOP
EEK!
PUT ME DOWN!
HOOU!
EEK!
OOF!
FLAP
HOOU!
HOOU!
FLAP
!
HOOU!
Get away- YOU DEVIL!
KIYA!
SMAK
?!
HOOU!

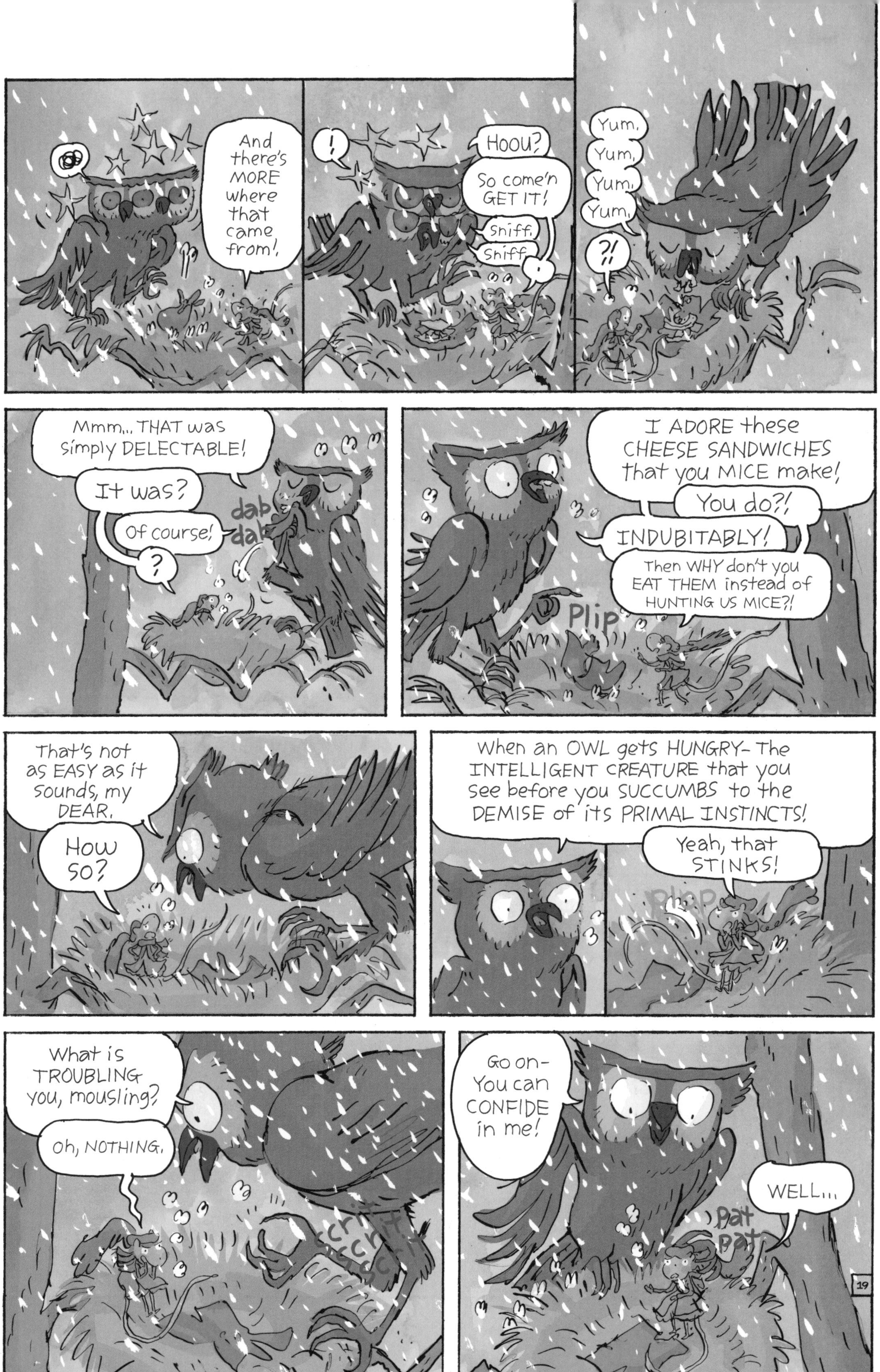
!
And there's MORE where that came from!
!
Hoou?
So come'n GET IT!
Sniff,
Sniff
Yum,
Yum,
Yum,
Yum,
?!
Mmm... THAT was simply DELECTABLE!
It was?
Of course!
?
dab
dab
I ADORE these CHEESE SANDWICHES that you MICE make!
You do?!
INDUBITABLY!
Then WHY don't you EAT THEM instead of HUNTING US MICE?!
Plip
That's not as EASY as it sounds, my DEAR.
How so?
When an OWL gets HUNGRY- The INTELLIGENT CREATURE that you see before you SUCCUMBS to the DEMISE of its PRIMAL INSTINCTS!
Yeah, that STINKS!
What is TROUBLING you, mousling?
Oh, NOTHING.
Go on- You can CONFIDE in me!
WELL...
pat
pat

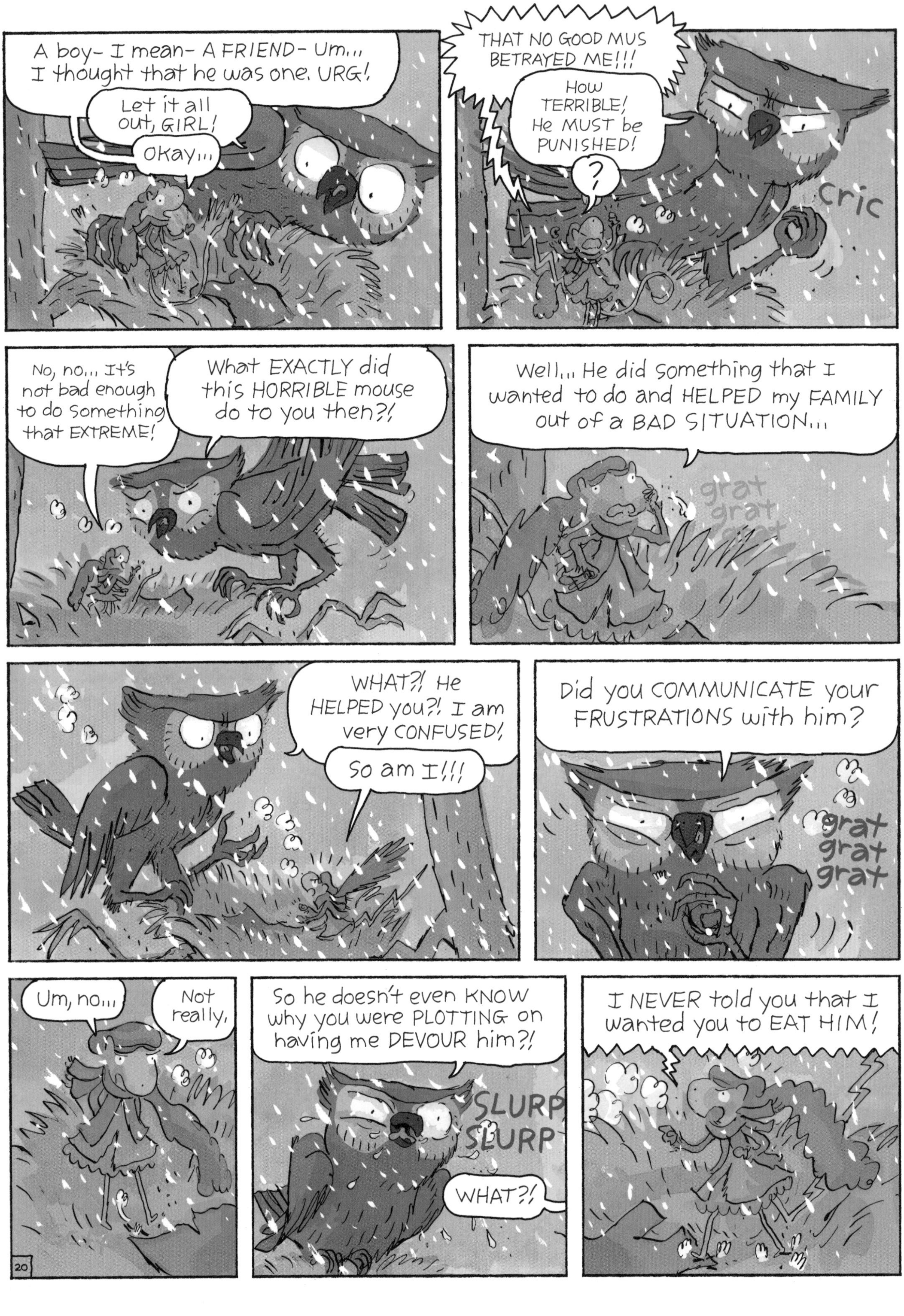

A boy- I mean- A FRIEND- Um...
I thought that he was one. URG!
Let it all out, GIRL!
Okay...
THAT NO GOOD MUS BETRAYED ME!!!
How TERRIBLE! He MUST be PUNISHED!
?
cric
No, no... It's not bad enough to do something that EXTREME!
What EXACTLY did this HORRIBLE mouse do to you then?!
Well... He did something that I wanted to do and HELPED my FAMILY out of a BAD SITUATION...
grat grat grat
WHAT?! He HELPED you?! I am very CONFUSED!
So am I!!!
Did you COMMUNICATE your FRUSTRATIONS with him?
grat grat grat
Um, no...
Not really.
So he doesn't even KNOW why you were PLOTTING on having me DEVOUR him?!
SLURP SLURP
WHAT?!
I NEVER told you that I wanted you to EAT HIM!

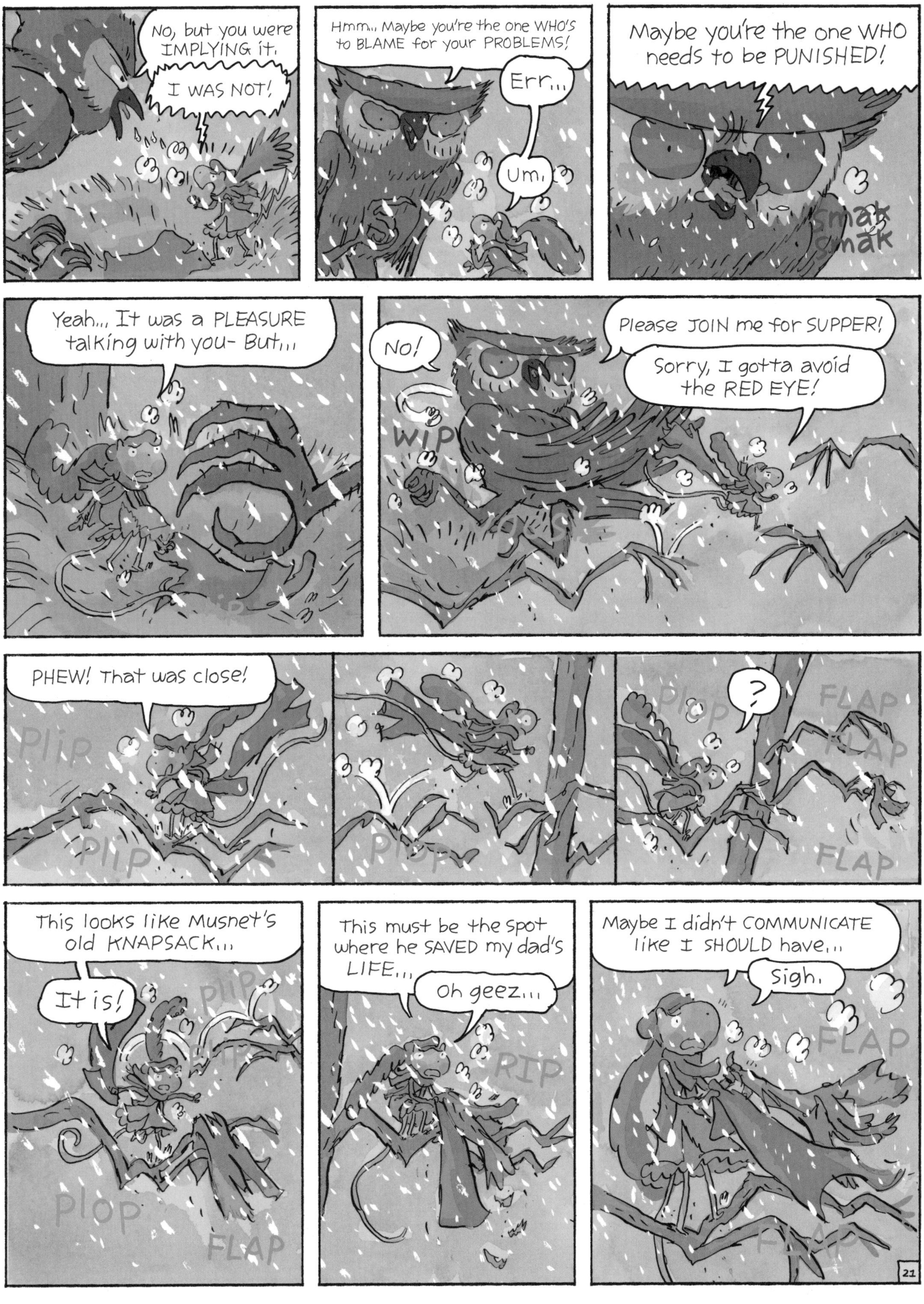

No, but you were IMPLYING it.
I WAS NOT!
Hmm... Maybe you're the one WHO'S to BLAME for your PROBLEMS!
Err...
Um.
Maybe you're the one WHO needs to be PUNISHED!
smak smak
Yeah... It was a PLEASURE talking with you- But...
No!
Please JOIN me for SUPPER!
Sorry, I gotta avoid the RED EYE!
WIP
PHEW! That was close!
Plip
Plip
Plop
?
Plop
FLAP
FLAP
FLAP
This looks like Musnet's old KNAPSACK...
It is!
plip
plip
Plop
FLAP
This must be the spot where he SAVED my dad's LIFE...
Oh geez...
RIP
Maybe I didn't COMMUNICATE like I SHOULD have...
Sigh.
FLAP
FLAP

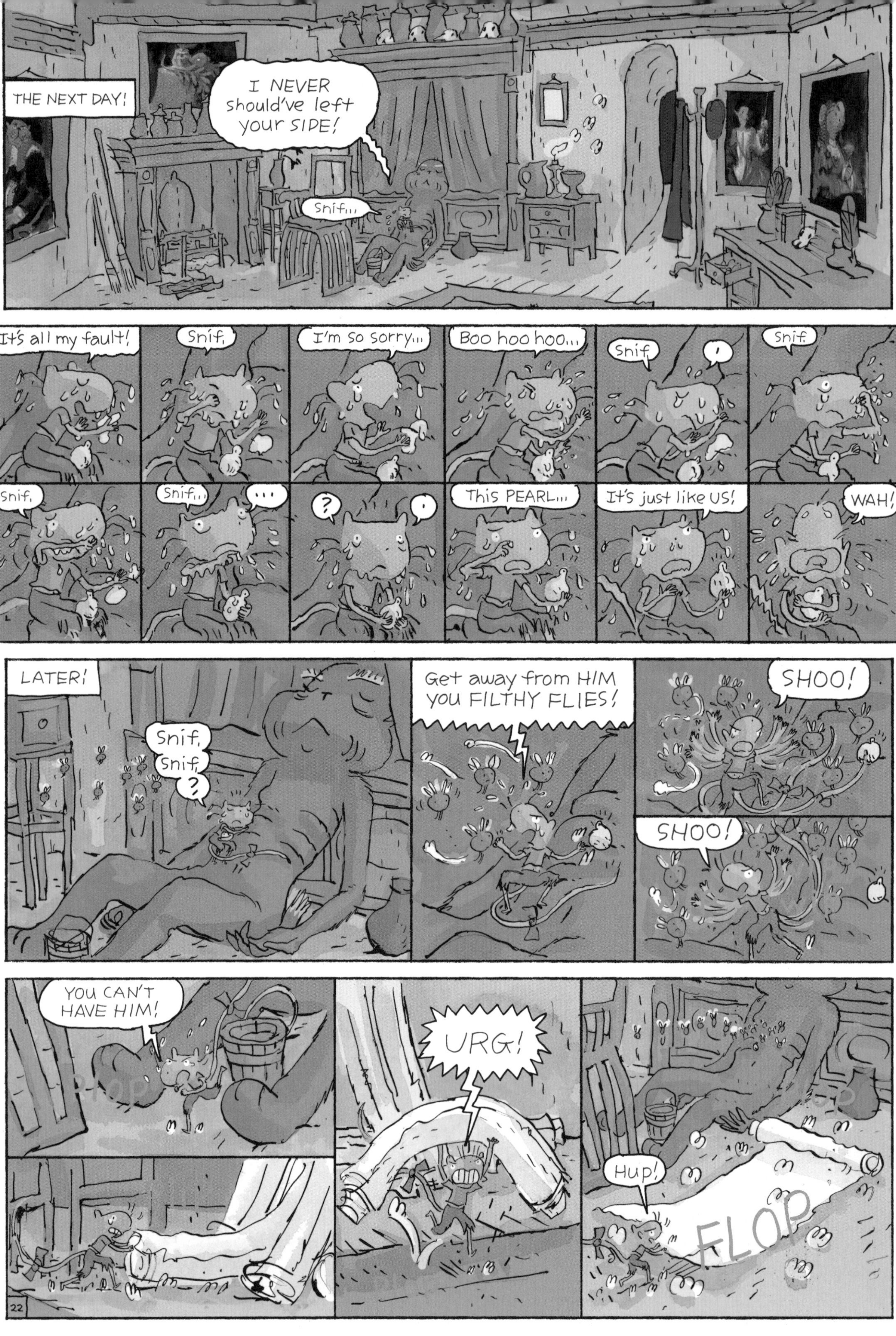
THE NEXT DAY!
I NEVER should've left your SIDE!
Snif...
It's all my fault!
Snif,
I'm so sorry...
Boo hoo hoo...
Snif,
!
Snif.
Snif,
Snif...
...
?
!
This PEARL...
It's just like US!
WAH!
LATER!
Snif,
snif,
?
Get away from HIM you FILTHY FLIES!
SHOO!
SHOO!
YOU CAN'T HAVE HIM!
URG!
Hup!
FLOP

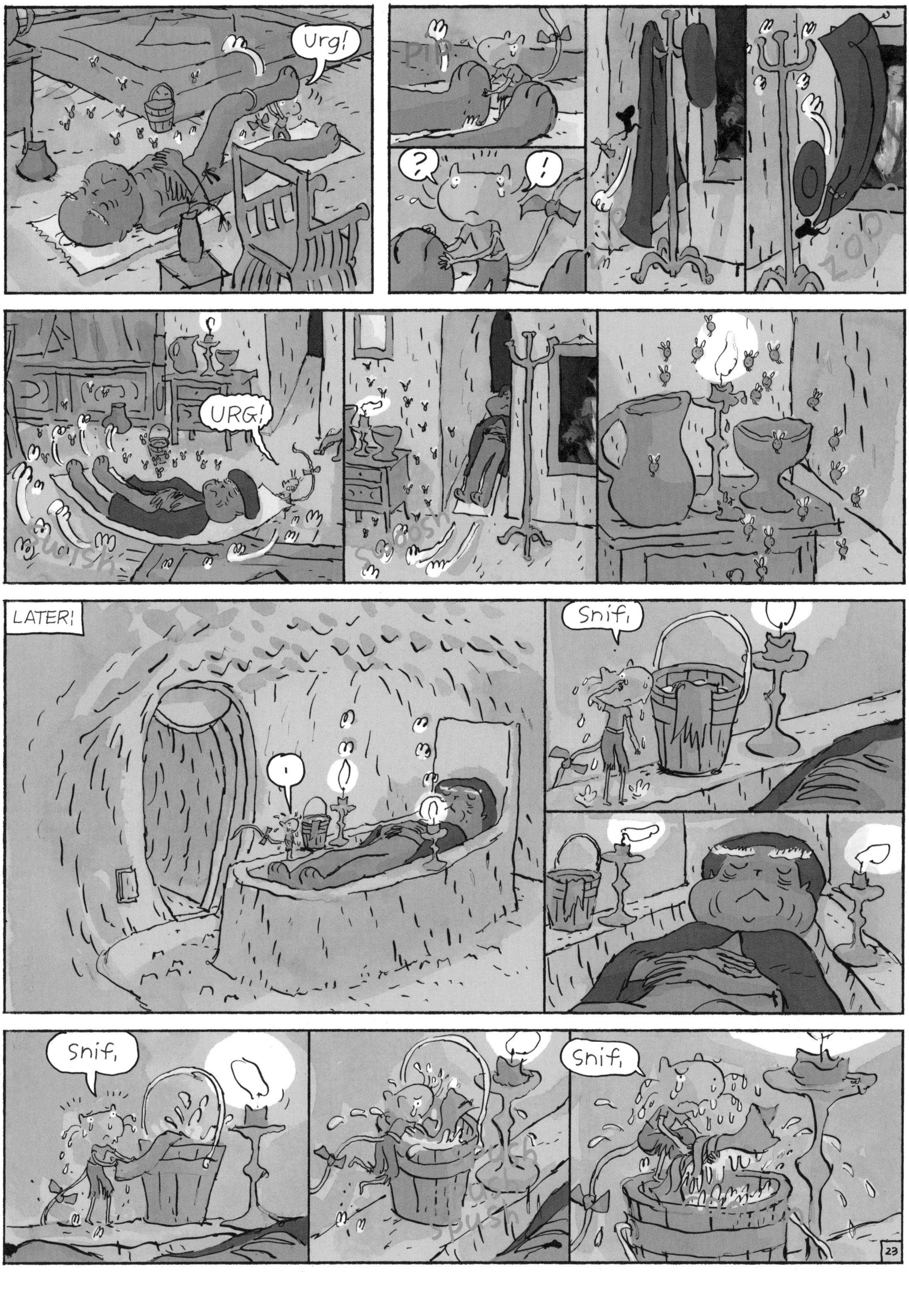
Urg!
pip
?
!
zop
URG!
swish
swoosh
LATER!
!
Snif,
Snif,
Snif,
spush

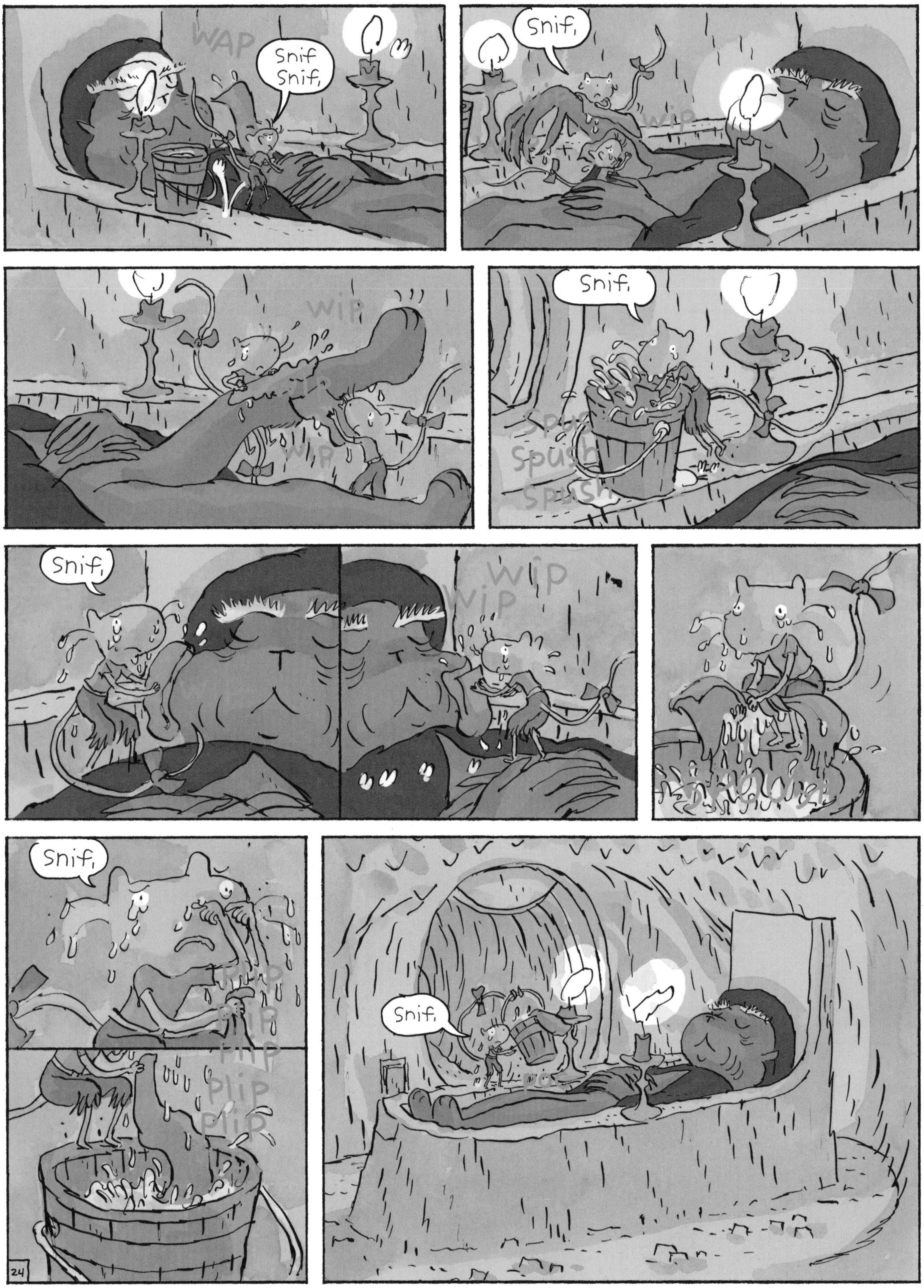
WAP
Snif
Snif,
Snif,
wip
wip
wip
plip
wip
Snif,
Spush
Spush
Spush
Snif,
wip
wip
Snif,
Plip
Plip
Plip
Plip
Plip
Snif,

PLOP

Snif,

I...

I CAN'T DO IT!

WOOOOOOVV

Huh?!

TONK

PLUVK

ALL RIGHT!

WHO'S THERE?!

Come on out and show YOURSELF!

WOOOOOOVV

?!

WOOOOOOOVV

EEEEEEEK!

WOOOOOOOVV

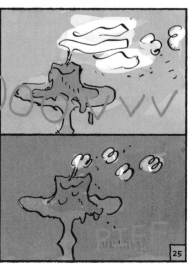

SOON;

BAM
BAM
BAM

火
？！

Long time no SEE, AMI!

ハハ！

What do you THINK of the NEW BUNKBED that I made for US?

?

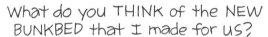

What's the matter MUSNET?!

N-N-NOTHING!

Well, you'd better start getting DRESSED—The BRIESOURIX'S CHEESEMAS PARTY is tonight!

NO.

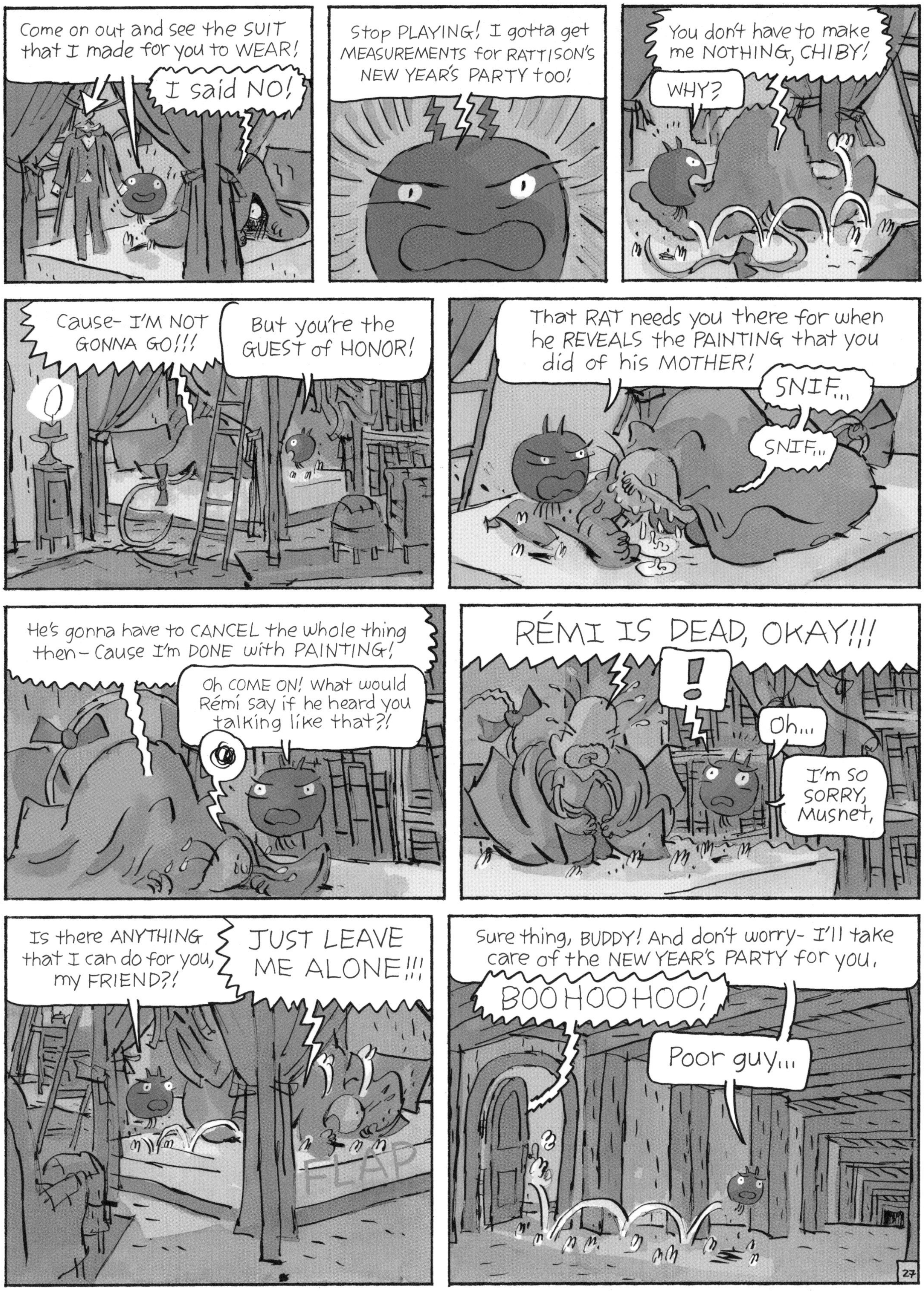

Come on out and see the SUIT that I made for you to WEAR!
I said NO!
Stop PLAYING! I gotta get MEASUREMENTS for RATTISON'S NEW YEAR'S PARTY too!
You don't have to make me NOTHING, CHIBY!
WHY?
Cause- I'M NOT GONNA GO!!!
But you're the GUEST of HONOR!
That RAT needs you there for when he REVEALS the PAINTING that you did of his MOTHER!
SNIF...
SNIF...
He's gonna have to CANCEL the whole thing then- Cause I'm DONE with PAINTING!
Oh COME ON! What would Rémi say if he heard you talking like that?!
RÉMI IS DEAD, OKAY!!!
!
Oh...
I'm SO SORRY, Musnet.
Is there ANYTHING that I can do for you, my FRIEND?!
JUST LEAVE ME ALONE!!!
FLAP
Sure thing, BUDDY! And don't worry- I'll take care of the NEW YEAR'S PARTY for you.
BOO HOO HOO!
Poor guy...

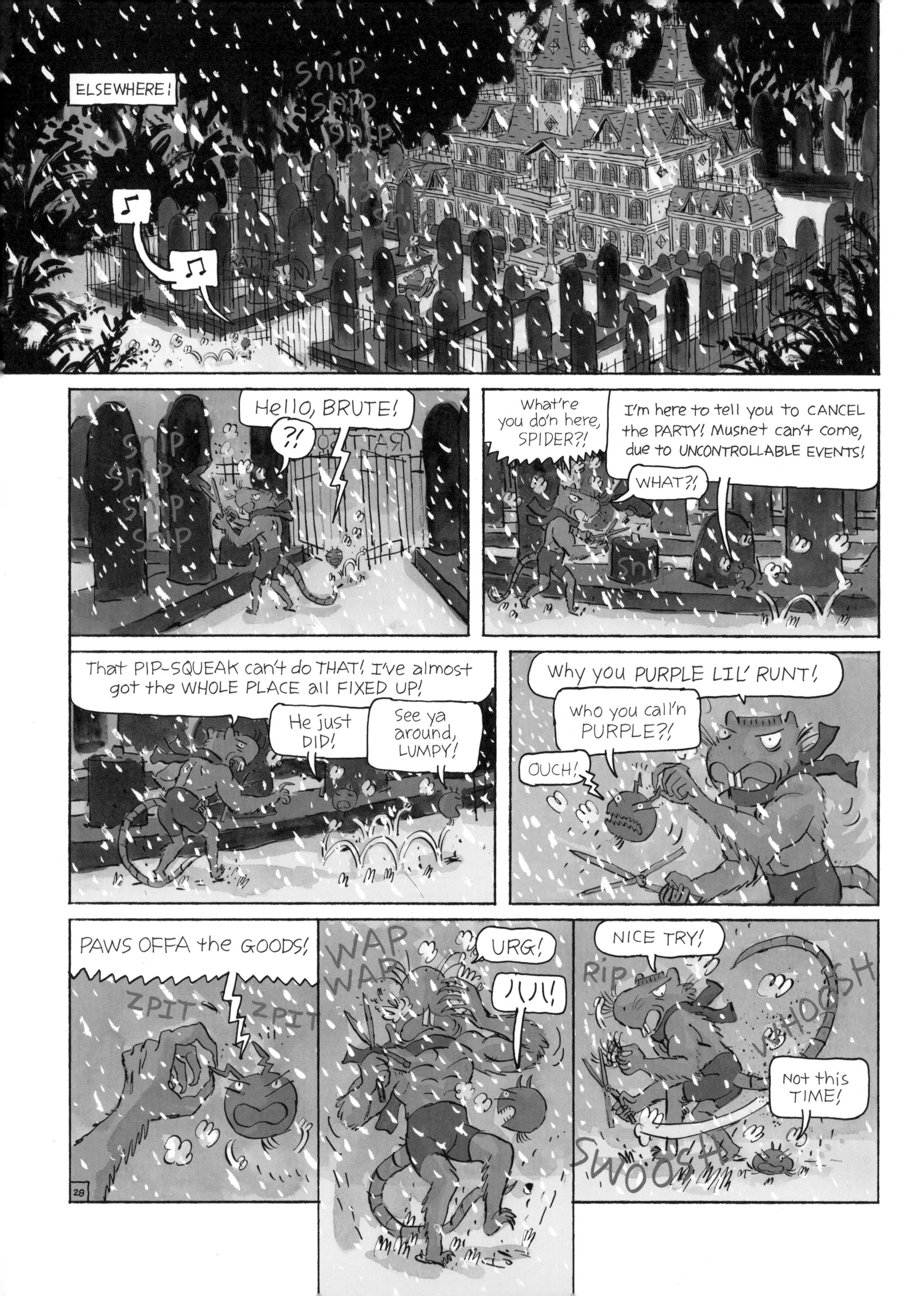
ELSEWHERE!
snip
snip
snip
snip
snip
Hello, BRUTE!
?!
snip
snip
snip
snip
What're you do'n here, SPIDER?!
I'm here to tell you to CANCEL the PARTY! Musnet can't come, due to UNCONTROLLABLE EVENTS!
WHAT?!
That PIP-SQUEAK can't do THAT! I've almost got the WHOLE PLACE all FIXED UP!
He just DID!
See ya around, LUMPY!
Why you PURPLE LIL' RUNT!
Who you call'n PURPLE?!
OUCH!
PAWS OFFA the GOODS!
ZPIT
ZPIT
28
WAP
WAP
URG!
NICE TRY!
RIP
WHOOSH
Not this TIME!
SWOOSH

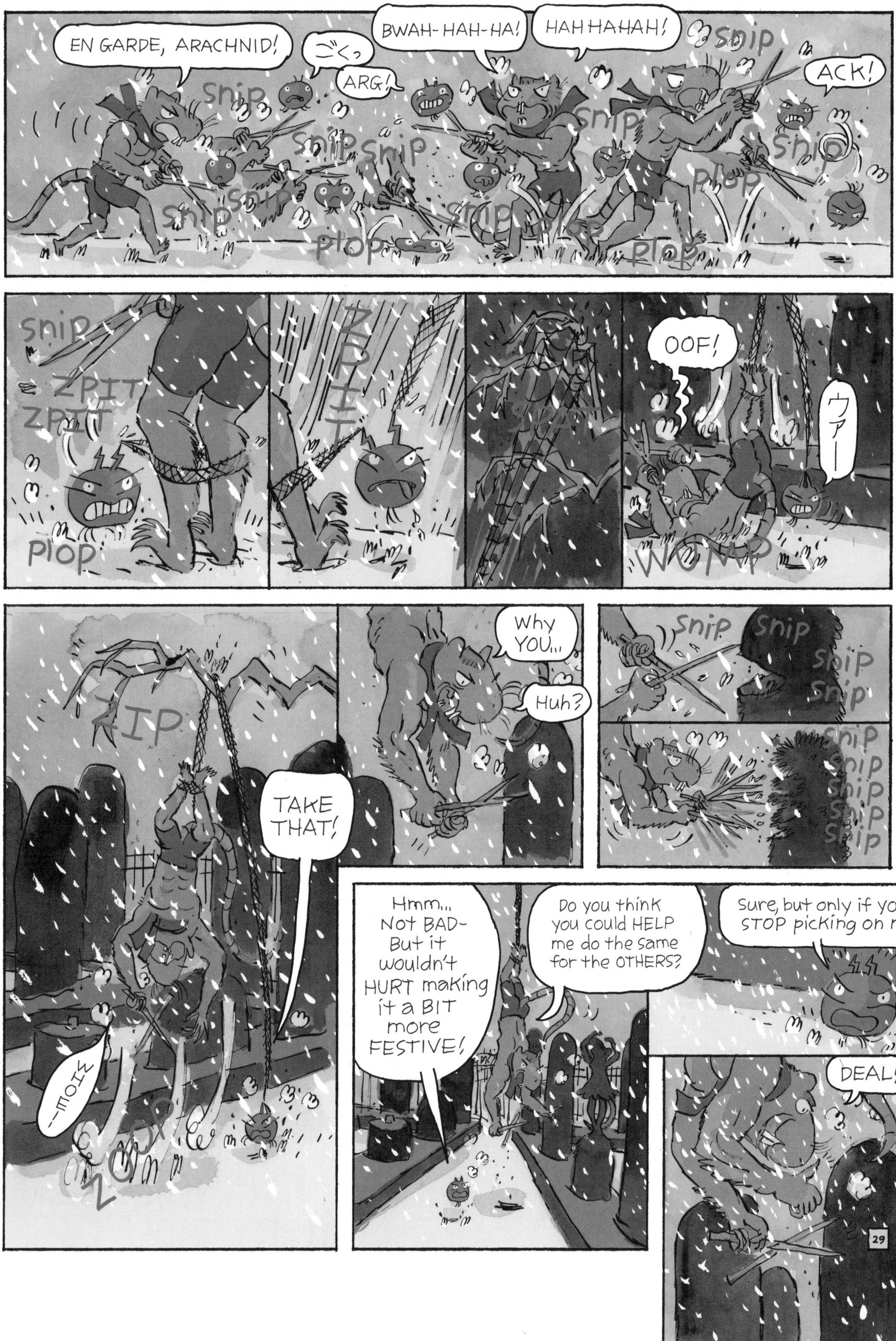
EN GARDE, ARACHNID!
ごくっ
ARG!
BWAH-HAH-HA!
HAH HAHAH!
ACK!
snip
plop
ZPIT
ZPIT
OOF!
ウァー
WOMP
ZIP
TAKE THAT!
Why YOU...
Huh?
snip
Hmm... Not BAD- But it wouldn't HURT making it a BIT more FESTIVE!
Do you think you could HELP me do the same for the OTHERS?
Sure, but only if you'll STOP picking on me!
DEAL!

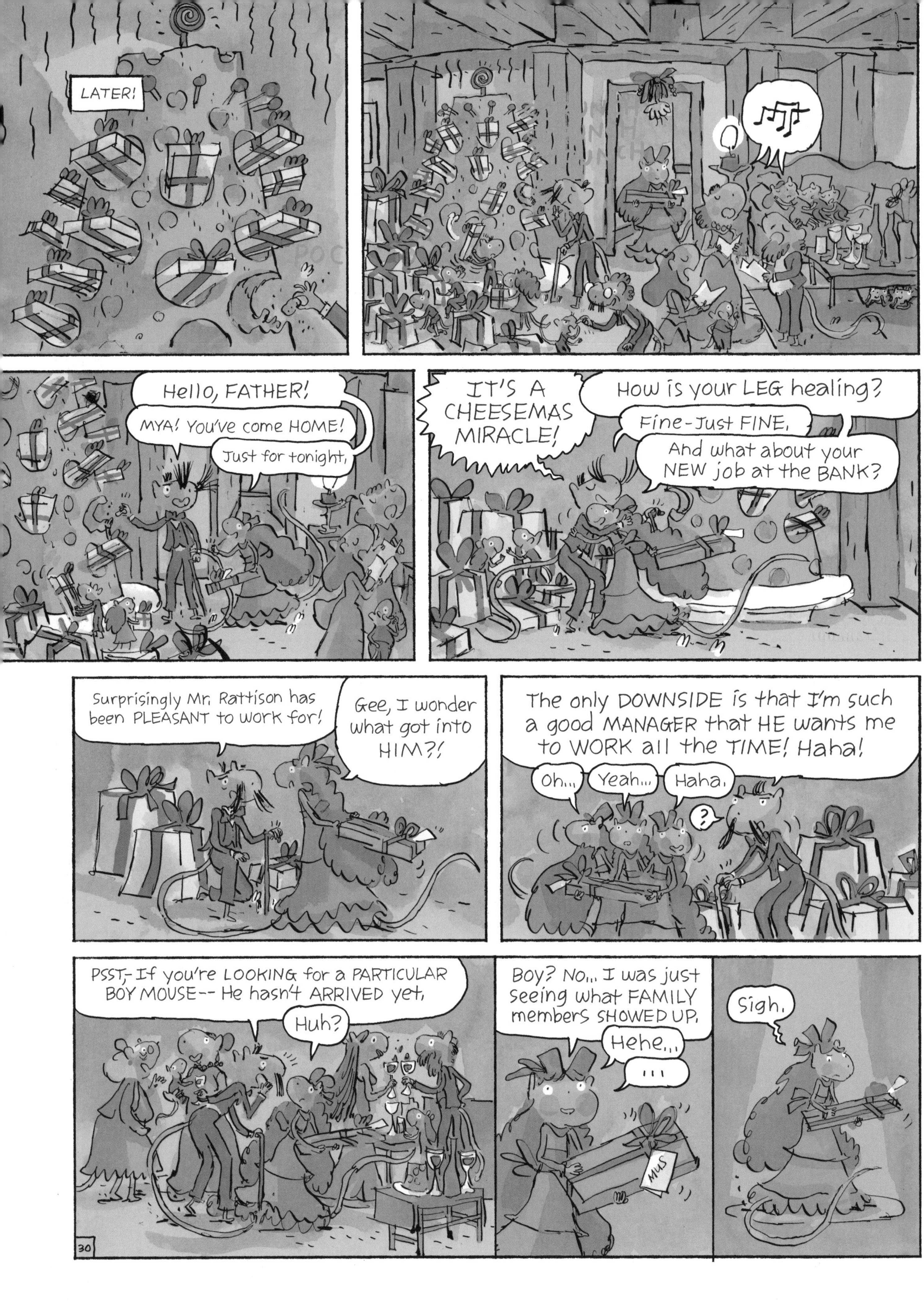
LATER!
Hello, FATHER!
MYA! You've come HOME!
Just for tonight.
IT'S A CHEESEMAS MIRACLE!
How is your LEG healing?
Fine-Just FINE.
And what about your NEW job at the BANK?
Surprisingly Mr. Rattison has been PLEASANT to work for!
Gee, I wonder what got into HIM?!
The only DOWNSIDE is that I'm such a good MANAGER that HE wants me to WORK all the TIME! Haha!
Oh...
Yeah...
Haha.
?
PSST,- If you're LOOKING for a PARTICULAR BOY MOUSE-- He hasn't ARRIVED yet.
Huh?
Boy? No... I was just seeing what FAMILY members SHOWED UP.
Hehe...
...
MUS
Sigh.

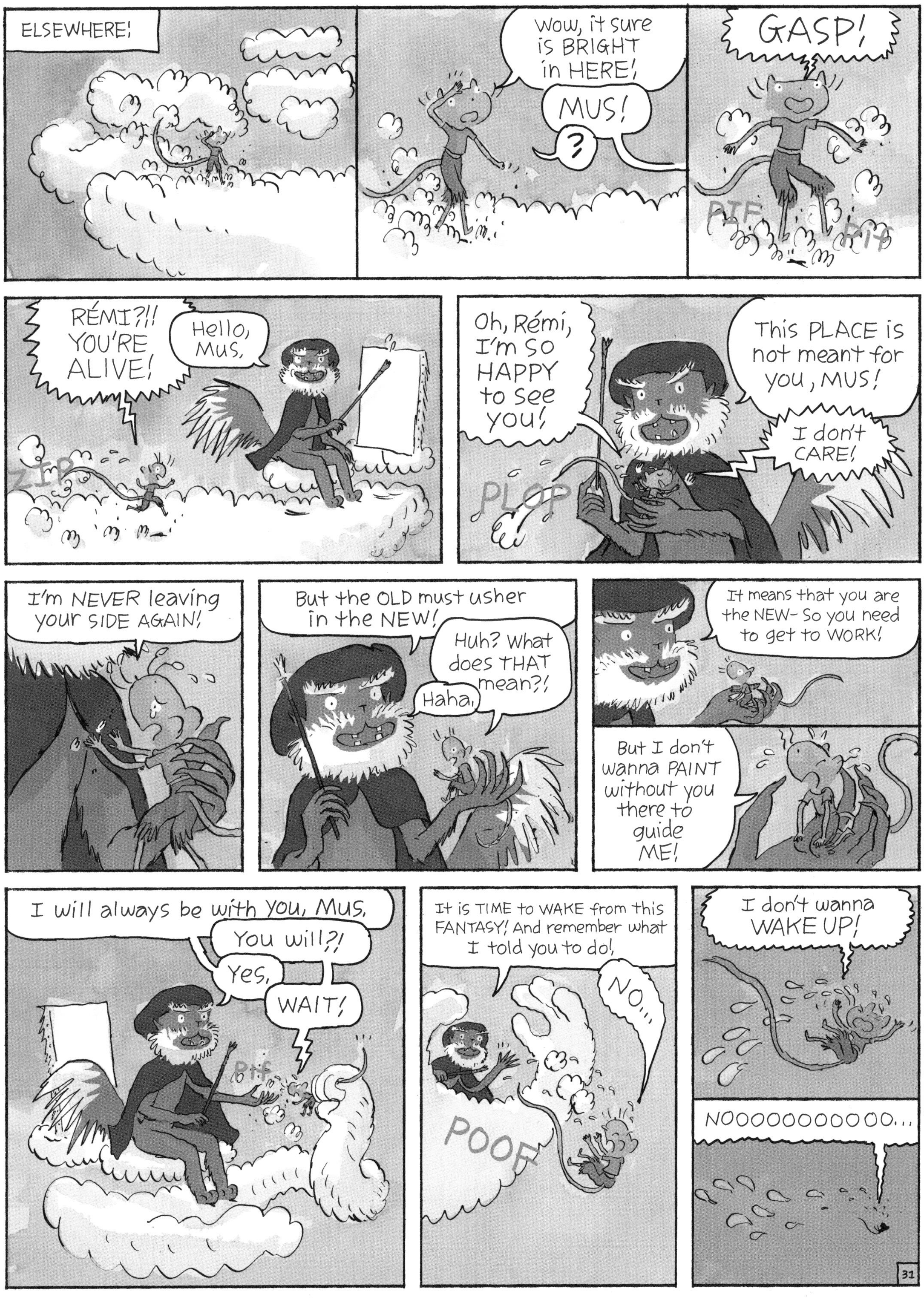
ELSEWHERE!
Wow, it sure is BRIGHT in HERE!
MUS!
?
GASP!
PIF
PIF
RÉMI?!! YOU'RE ALIVE!
Hello, Mus.
ZIP
Oh, Rémi, I'm SO HAPPY to see you!
This PLACE is not meant for you, MUS!
I don't CARE!
PLOP
I'm NEVER leaving your SIDE AGAIN!
But the OLD must usher in the NEW!
Huh? What does THAT mean?!
Haha.
It means that you are the NEW- So you need to get to WORK!
But I don't wanna PAINT without you there to guide ME!
I will always be with you, Mus.
You will?!
Yes.
WAIT!
PIF
It is TIME to WAKE from this FANTASY! And remember what I told you to do!
NO...
POOF
I don't wanna WAKE UP!
NOOOOOOOOOOO...

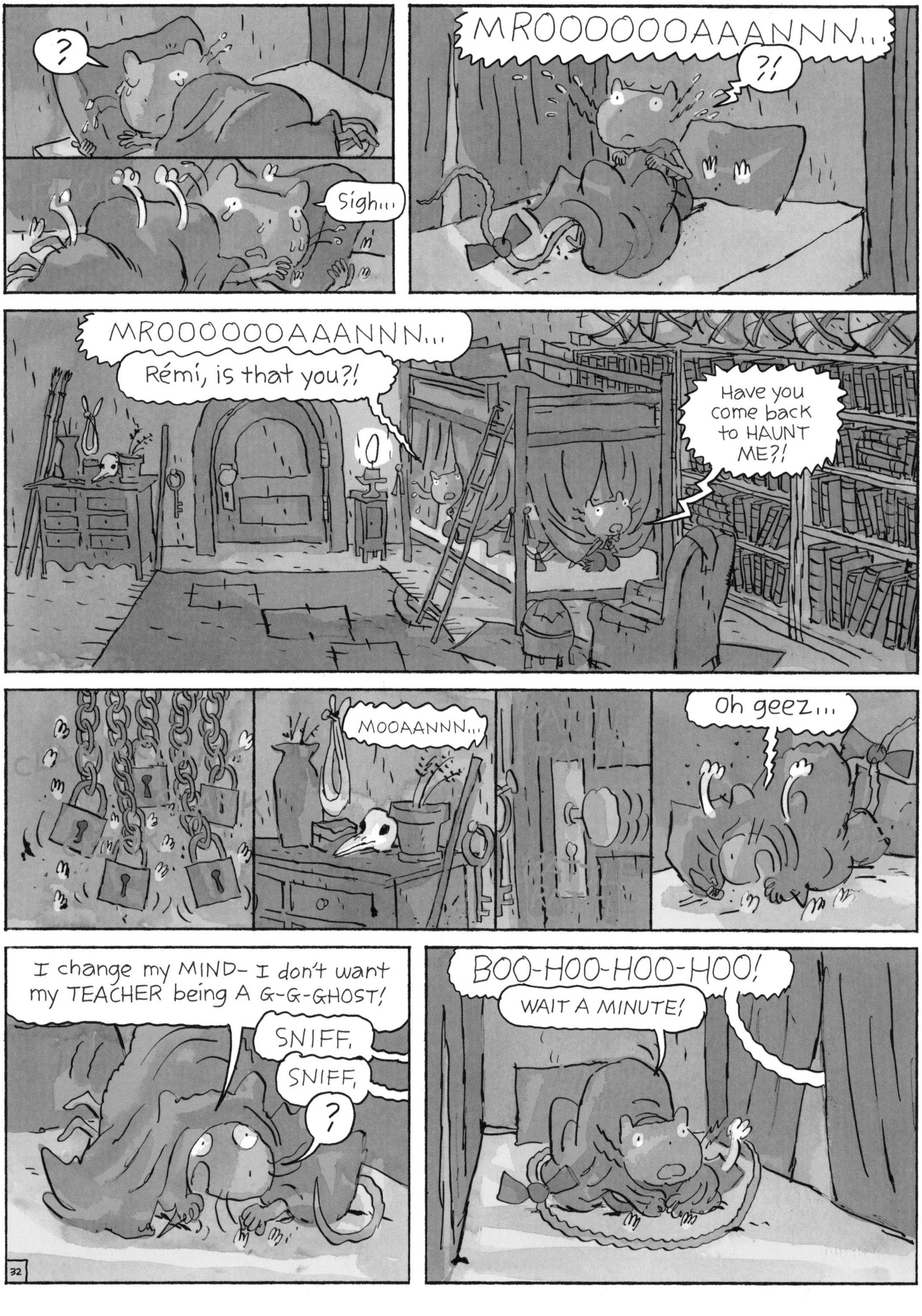
?
Sigh...
MROOOOOOAAANNN...
?!
MROOOOOOAAANNN...
Rémi, is that you?!
Have you come back to HAUNT ME?!
MOOAANNN...
Oh geez...
I change my MIND- I don't want my TEACHER being A G-G-GHOST!
SNIFF,
SNIFF,
?
BOO-HOO-HOO-HOO!
WAIT A MINUTE!

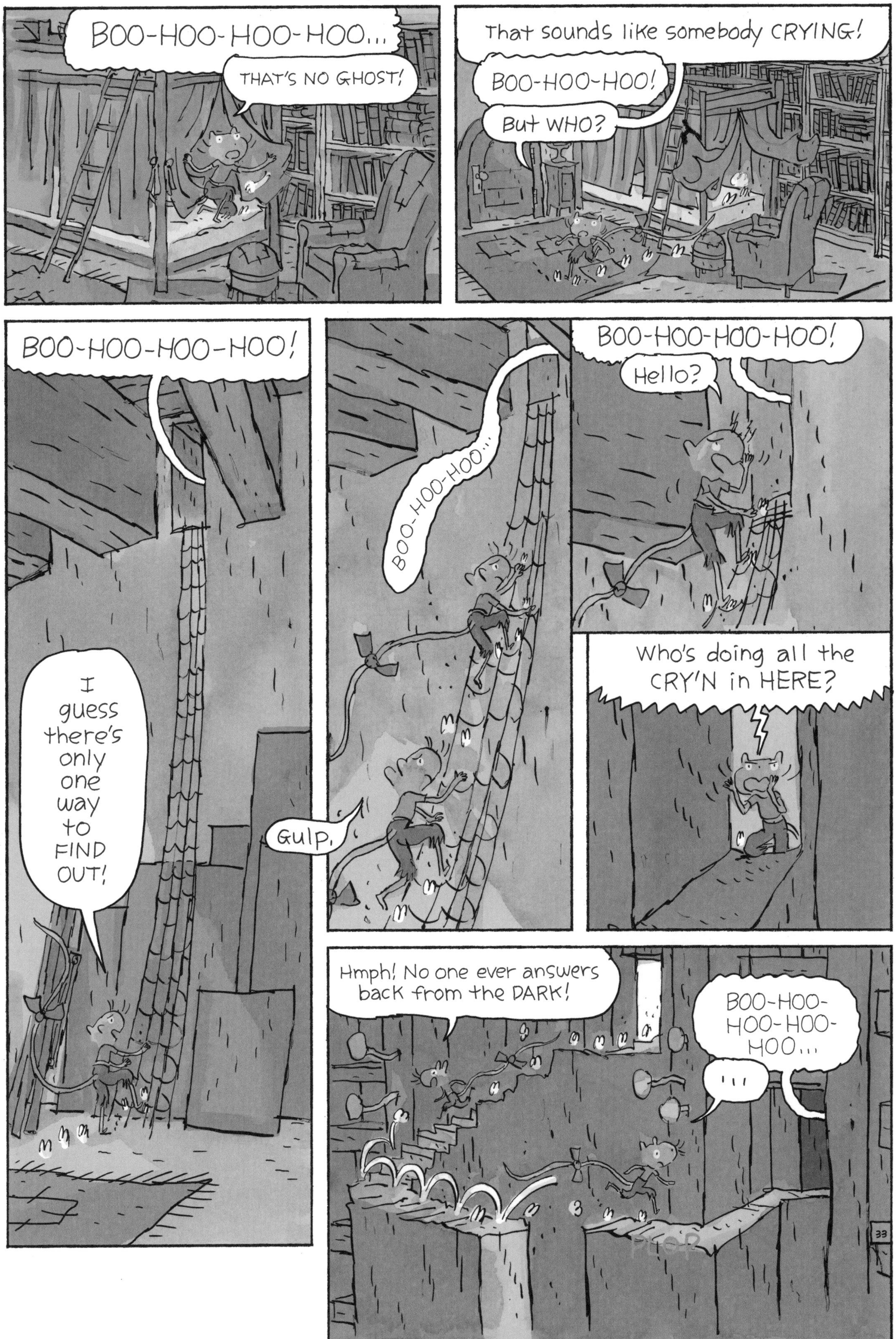
BOO-HOO-HOO-HOO...
THAT'S NO GHOST!
That sounds like somebody CRYING!
BOO-HOO-HOO!
But WHO?
BOO-HOO-HOO-HOO!
I guess there's only one way to FIND OUT!
BOO-HOO-HOO...
Gulp.
BOO-HOO-HOO-HOO!
Hello?
Who's doing all the CRY'N in HERE?
Hmph! No one ever answers back from the DARK!
BOO-HOO-HOO-HOO-HOO...
...

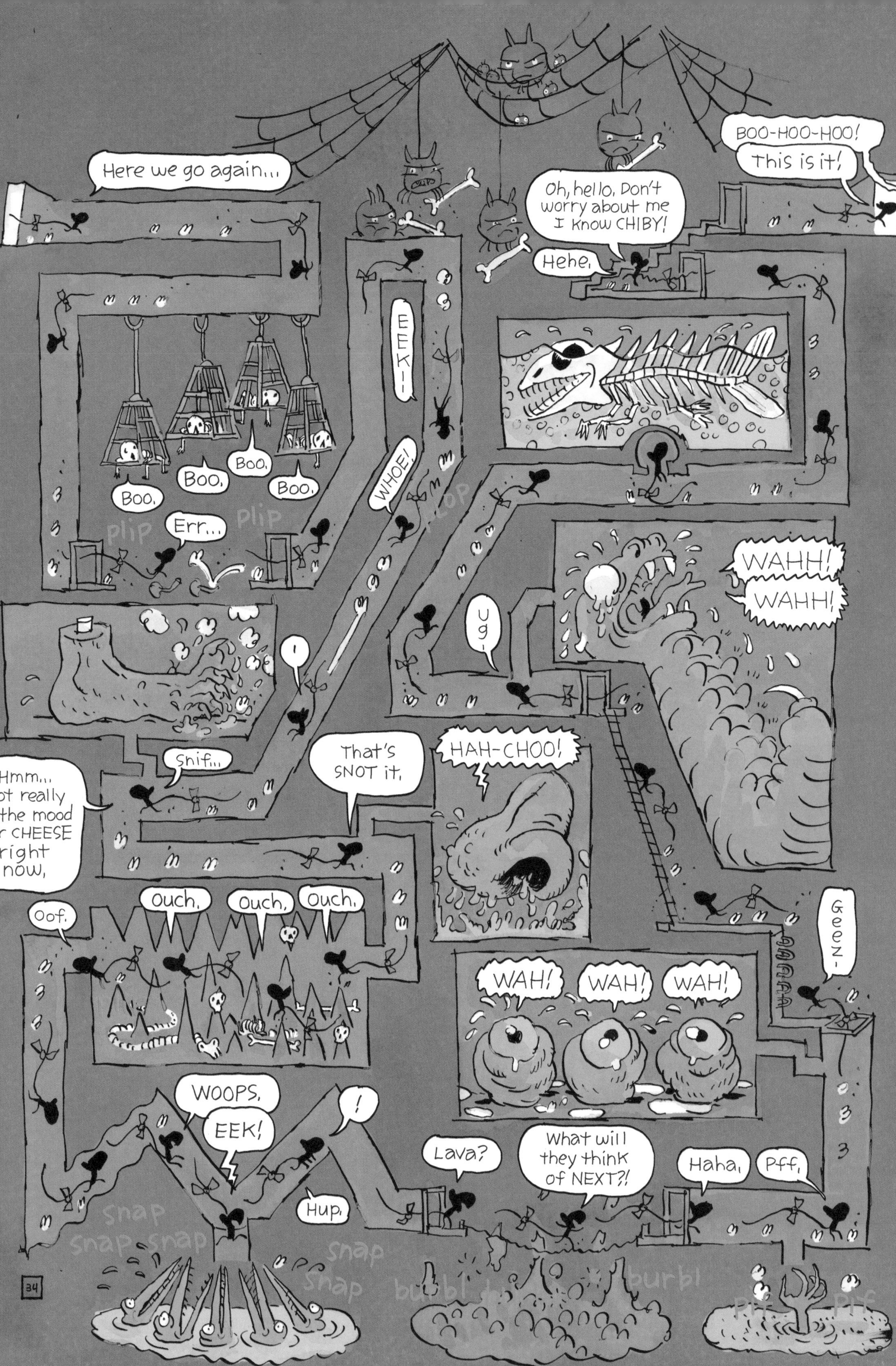

Here we go again...
Oh, hello. Don't worry about me I know CHIBY!
Hehe.
BOO-HOO-HOO!
This is it!
EEK!
Boo.
Boo.
Boo.
Boo.
Err...
plip
plip
WHOE!
Ug.
WAHH!
WAHH!
!
Snif...
Hmm... Not really in the mood for CHEESE right now.
That's SNOT it.
HAH-CHOO!
Geez.
Oof.
Ouch.
Ouch.
Ouch.
WAH!
WAH!
WAH!
WOOPS.
EEK!
!
Hup.
Lava?
What will they think of NEXT?!
Haha.
Pff.
snap
snap snap
snap
snap
burbl
burbl

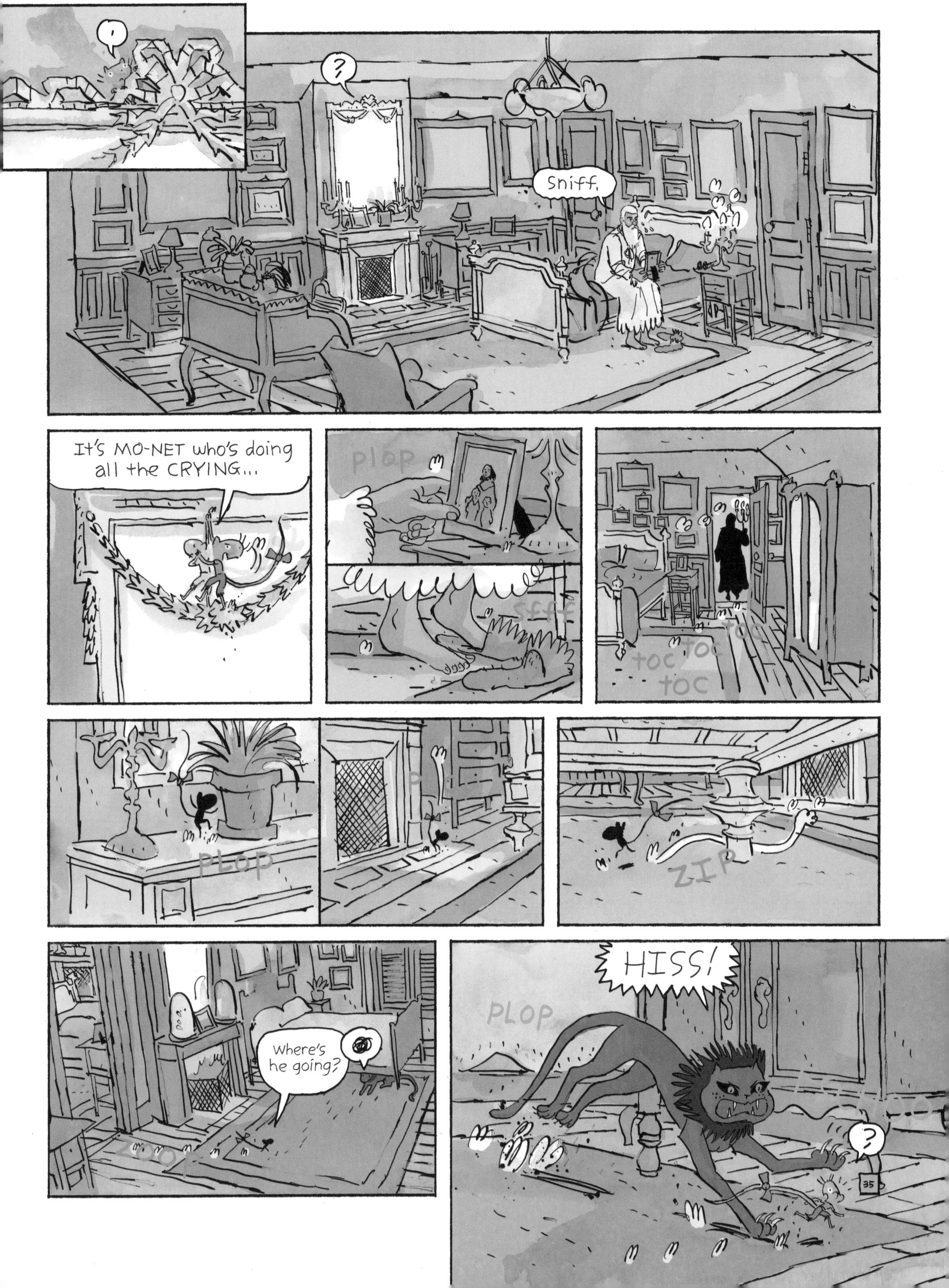
?
Sniff.
It's MO-NET who's doing all the CRYING...
PLOP
sfff
toc toc toc toc
PLOP
ZIP
Where's he going?
ZOOP
HISS!
PLOP
?
35

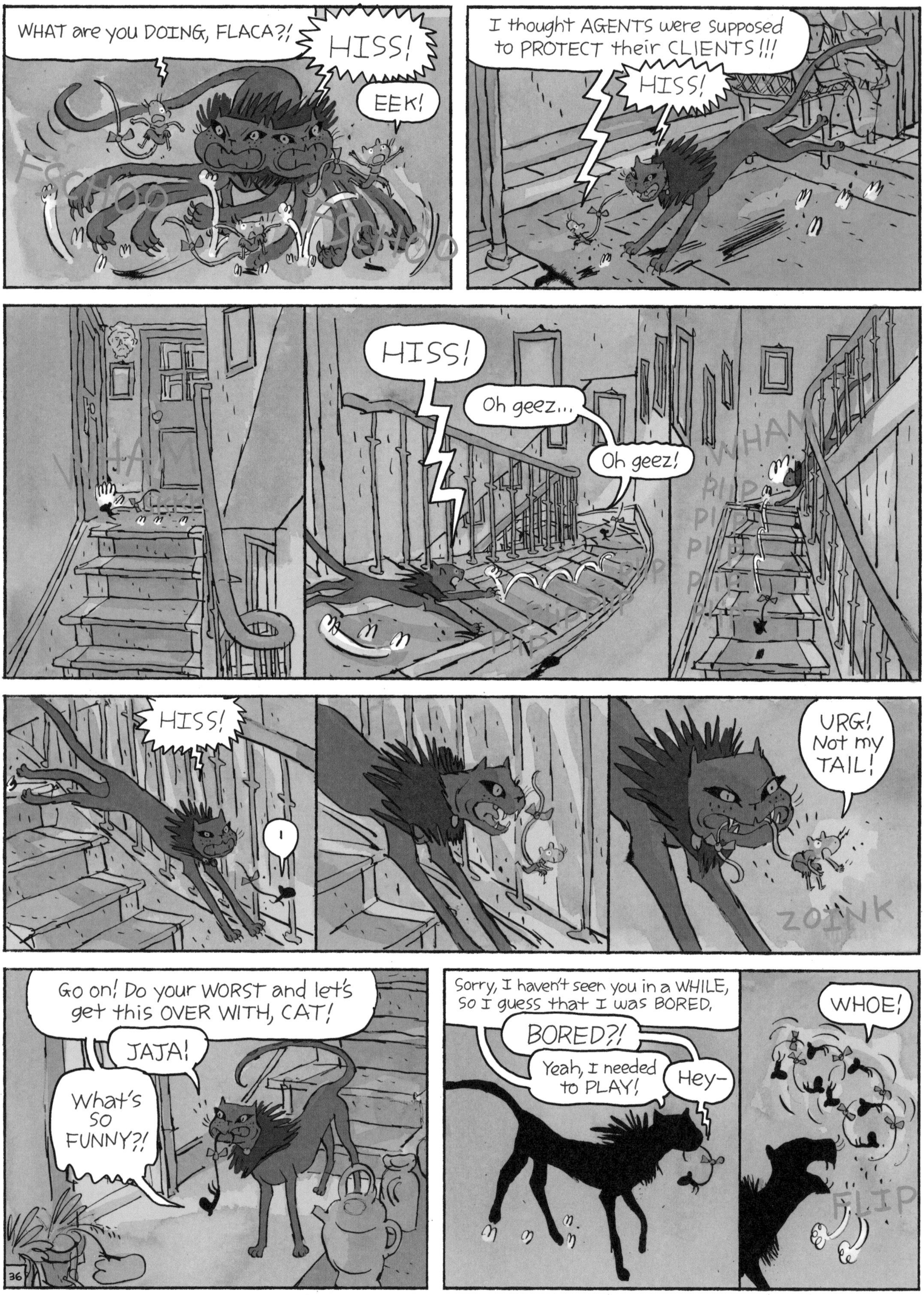
WHAT are you DOING, FLACA?!
HISS!
EEK!
FSCHOO
FSCHOO
I thought AGENTS were supposed to PROTECT their CLIENTS!!!
HISS!
WHAM
HISS!
Oh geez...
Oh geez!
WHAM
HISS!
!
URG! Not my TAIL!
ZOINK
Go on! Do your WORST and let's get this OVER WITH, CAT!
JAJA!
What's so FUNNY?!
Sorry, I haven't seen you in a WHILE, so I guess that I was BORED.
BORED?!
Yeah, I needed to PLAY!
Hey-
WHOE!
FLIP

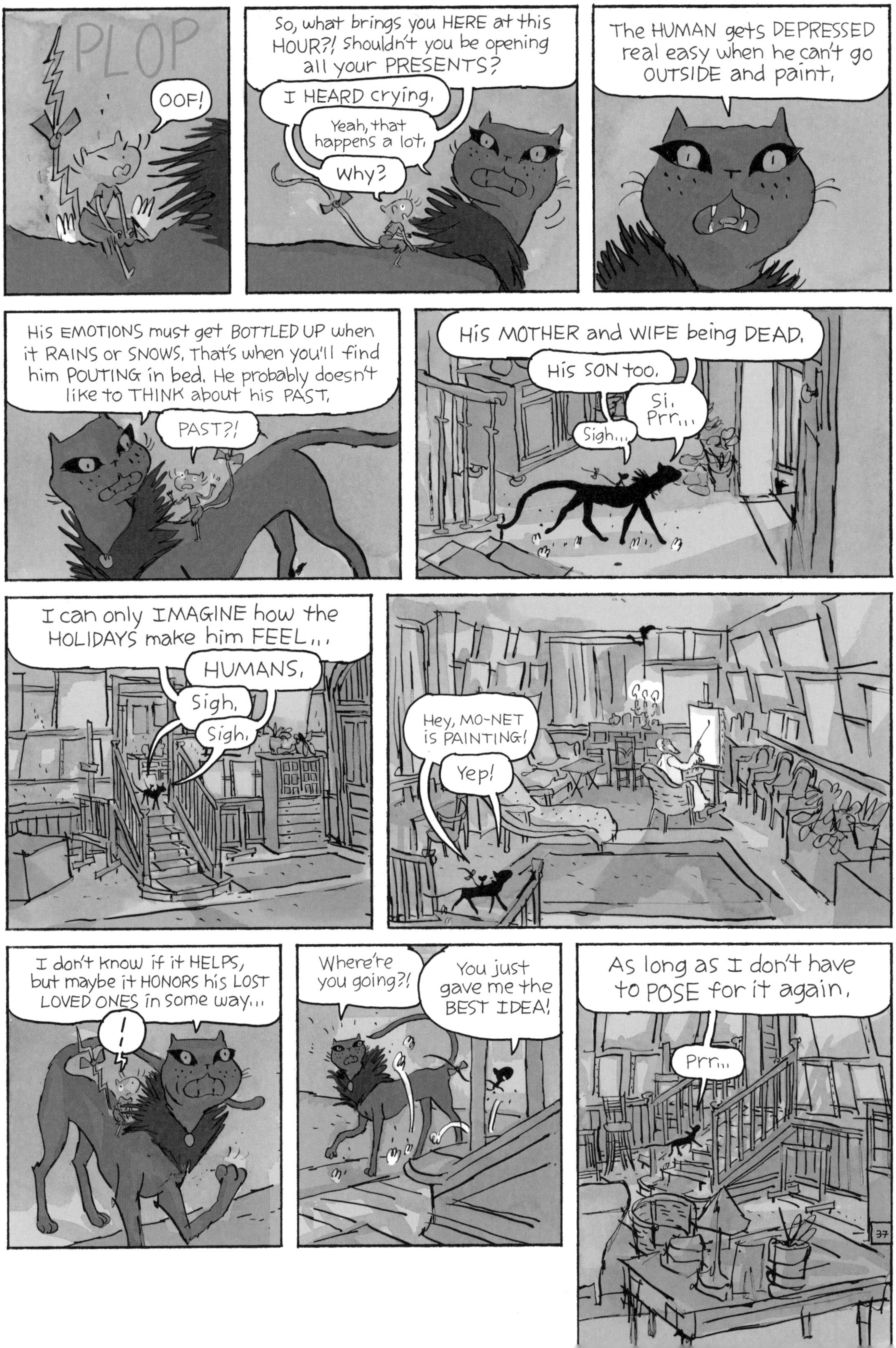
PLOP
OOF!
So, what brings you HERE at this HOUR?! Shouldn't you be opening all your PRESENTS?
I HEARD crying.
Yeah, that happens a lot.
Why?
The HUMAN gets DEPRESSED real easy when he can't go OUTSIDE and paint.
His EMOTIONS must get BOTTLED UP when it RAINS or SNOWS. That's when you'll find him POUTING in bed. He probably doesn't like to THINK about his PAST.
PAST?!
His MOTHER and WIFE being DEAD.
His SON too.
Si. Prr...
Sigh...
I can only IMAGINE how the HOLIDAYS make him FEEL...
HUMANS.
Sigh.
Sigh.
Hey, MO-NET is PAINTING!
Yep!
I don't know if it HELPS, but maybe it HONORS his LOST LOVED ONES in some way...
!
Where're you going?!
You just gave me the BEST IDEA!
As long as I don't have to POSE for it again.
Prr...
37

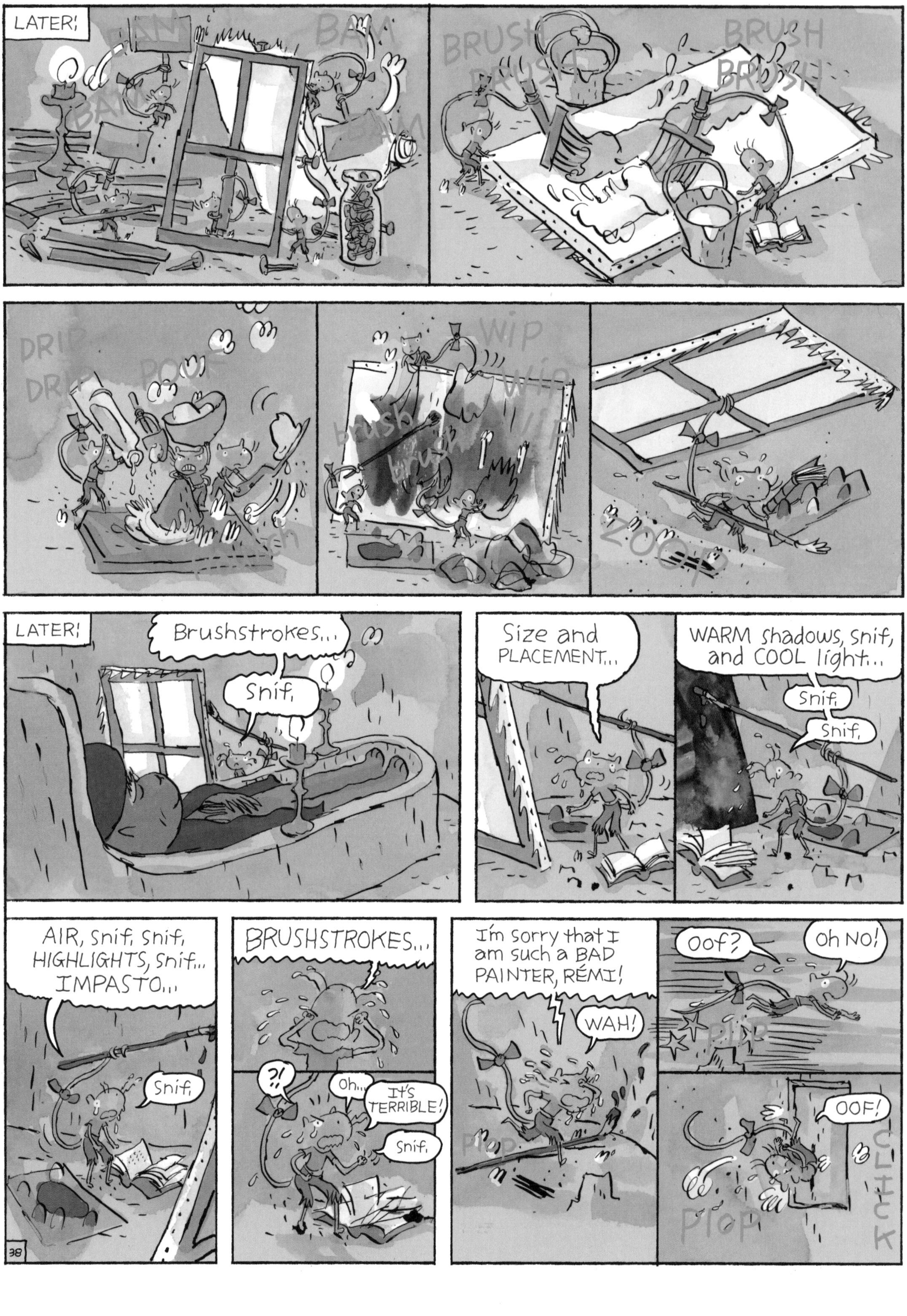
LATER!
BAM
BAM
BAM
BRUSH
BRUSH
BRUSH
BRUSH
DRIP
DRIP
POOF
WIP
WIP
WIP
brush
brush
ZOOP
LATER!
Brushstrokes...
Snif.
Size and PLACEMENT...
WARM shadows, snif, and COOL light...
Snif.
Snif.
AIR, snif, snif, HIGHLIGHTS, snif... IMPASTO...
Snif.
BRUSHSTROKES...
?!
Oh...
IT'S TERRIBLE!
Snif.
I'm sorry that I am such a BAD PAINTER, RÉMI!
WAH!
Plop
Oof?
Oh NO!
OOF!
Plop
CLICK

NO!

Oh, this is just GREAT!

I sealed myself in a TOMB!

OKAY, THINK, MUS! There's gotta be a way out that won't DISRESPECT this place—

WAIT— which way is NORTH?

This has to be it! Well, if I RUIN my TEETH, I'll just have to eat SOFT CHEESE!

SCRUNCH SCRUNCH SCRUNCH SCRUNCH

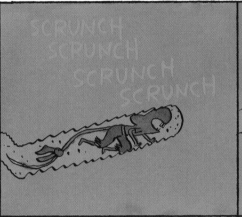

Scrunch Scrunch Scrunch

POP

I DID IT!

Urg!

PLOP

HUI TISCH

Hup!

I guess this is really GOODBYE my OLD FRIEND! I will never FORGET you.

Snif.

Oh GEEZ! I forgot my JOURNAL in there—

?!

JOURNAL!

That's right!

REMI'S STUDIO LIBRARY!

39

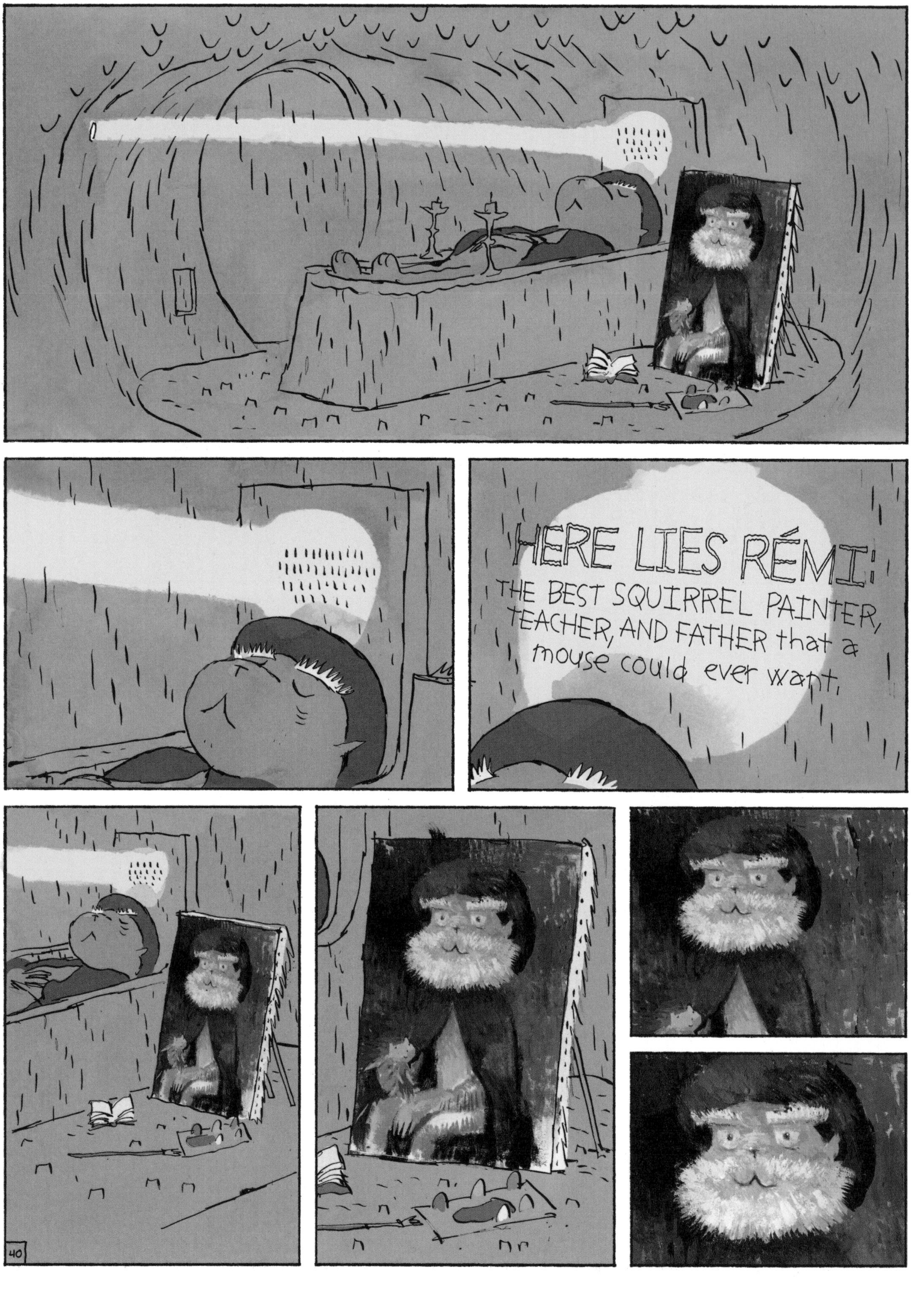
HERE LIES RÉMI:
THE BEST SQUIRREL PAINTER, TEACHER, AND FATHER that a mouse could ever want.
40

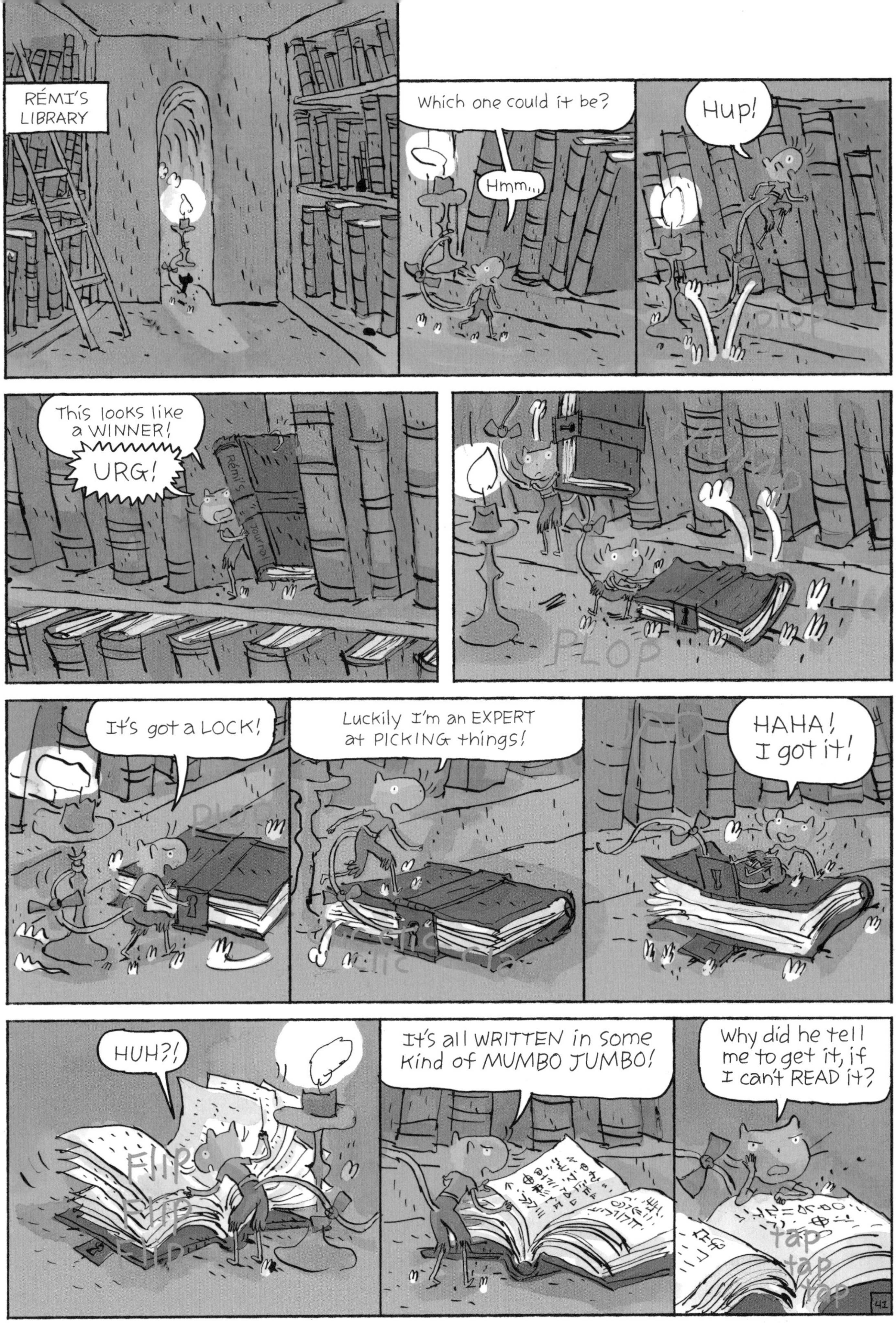
RÉMI'S LIBRARY
Which one could it be?
Hmm...
Hup!
PLOP
This looks like a WINNER!
URG!
Rémi's Journal
PLOP
It's got a LOCK!
Luckily I'm an EXPERT at PICKING things!
HAHA! I got it!
HUH?!
FLIP
FLIP
FLIP
It's all WRITTEN in some kind of MUMBO JUMBO!
Why did he tell me to get it, if I can't READ it?
tap
tap
tap

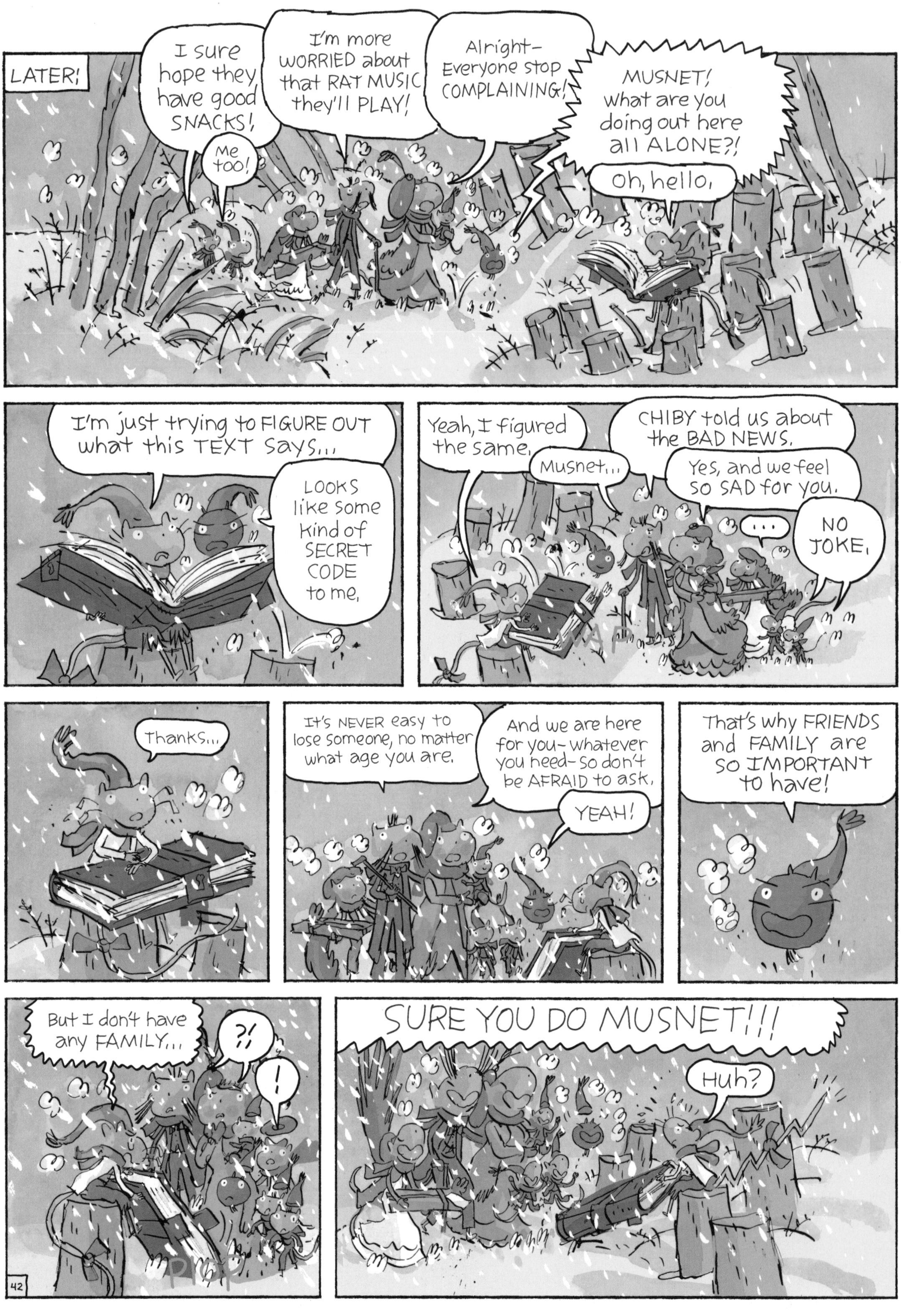
LATER.
I sure hope they have good SNACKS!
Me too!
I'm more WORRIED about that RAT MUSIC they'll PLAY!
Alright- Everyone stop COMPLAINING!
MUSNET! What are you doing out here all ALONE?!
Oh, hello.
I'm just trying to FIGURE OUT what this TEXT says...
LOOKS like some kind of SECRET CODE to me.
Yeah, I figured the same.
Musnet...
CHIBY told us about the BAD NEWS.
Yes, and we feel so SAD for you.
...
NO JOKE.
Thanks...
It's NEVER easy to lose someone, no matter what age you are.
And we are here for you- whatever you need- so don't be AFRAID to ask.
YEAH!
That's why FRIENDS and FAMILY are SO IMPORTANT to have!
But I don't have any FAMILY...
?!
!
SURE YOU DO MUSNET!!!
Huh?

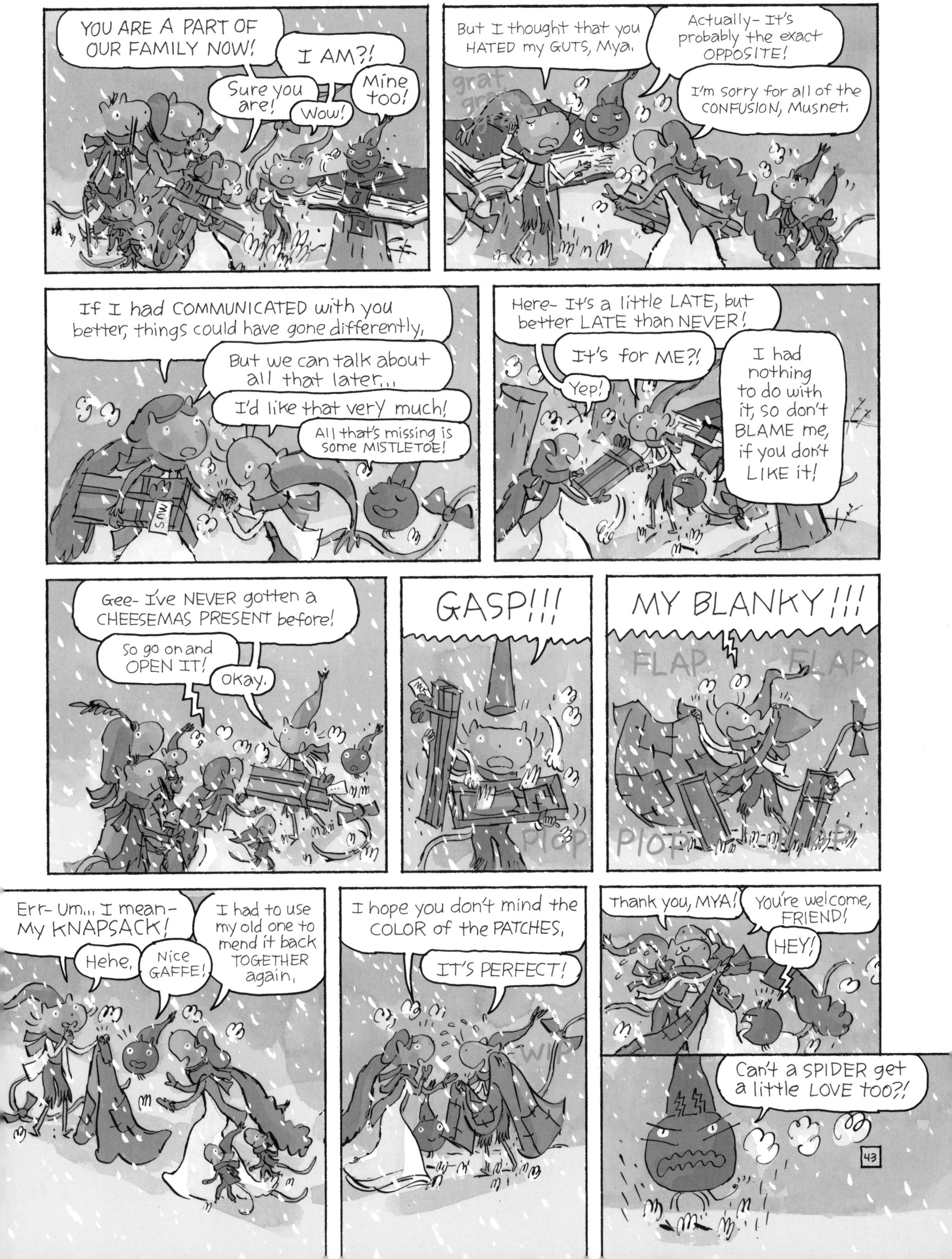
YOU ARE A PART OF OUR FAMILY NOW!
I AM?!
Sure you are!
Wow!
Mine too!
But I thought that you HATED my GUTS, Mya.
Actually- It's probably the exact OPPOSITE!
I'm sorry for all of the CONFUSION, Musnet.
If I had COMMUNICATED with you better, things could have gone differently.
But we can talk about all that later...
I'd like that very much!
All that's missing is some MISTLETOE!
MUS
Here- It's a little LATE, but better LATE than NEVER!
It's for ME?!
Yep!
I had nothing to do with it, so don't BLAME me, if you don't LIKE it!
Gee- I've NEVER gotten a CHEESEMAS PRESENT before!
So go on and OPEN IT!
Okay.
GASP!!!
MY BLANKY!!!
FLAP FLAP
Err- Um... I mean- My KNAPSACK!
Hehe.
Nice GAFFE!
I had to use my old one to mend it back TOGETHER again.
I hope you don't mind the COLOR of the PATCHES.
IT'S PERFECT!
Thank you, MYA!
You're welcome, FRIEND!
HEY!
Can't a SPIDER get a little LOVE too?!

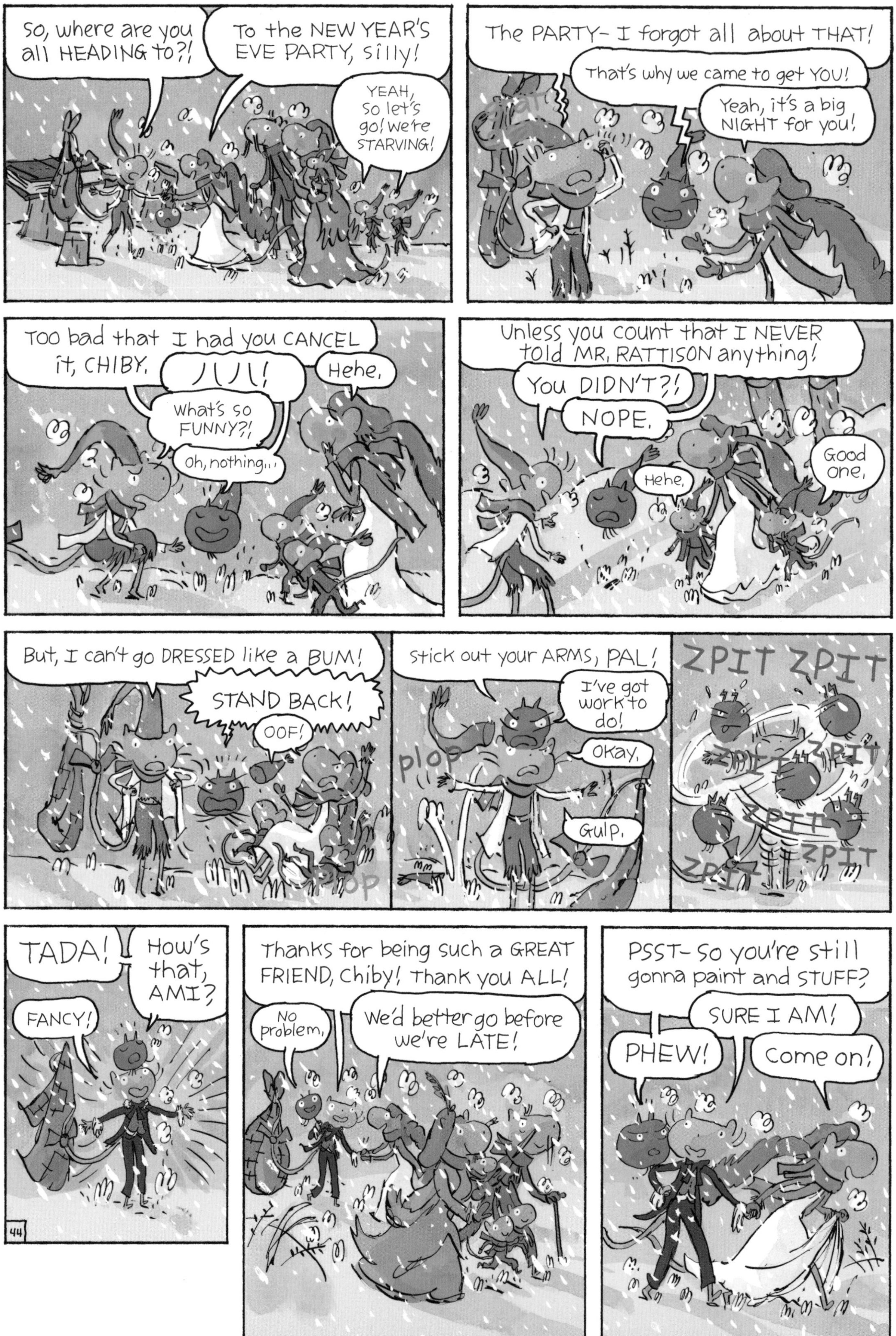
So, where are you all HEADING to?!
To the NEW YEAR'S EVE PARTY, silly!
YEAH, so let's go! We're STARVING!
The PARTY- I forgot all about THAT!
That's why we came to get YOU!
Yeah, it's a big NIGHT for you!
TOO bad that I had you CANCEL it, CHIBY.
ハハ!
Hehe.
What's so FUNNY?!
Oh, nothing...
Unless you count that I NEVER told MR. RATTISON anything!
You DIDN'T?!
NOPE.
Hehe.
Good one.
But, I can't go DRESSED like a BUM!
STAND BACK!
OOF!
plop
Stick out your ARMS, PAL!
I've got work to do!
plop
Okay.
Gulp.
ZPIT ZPIT
ZPIT ZPIT
ZPIT
ZPIT
ZPIT
TADA!
How's that, AMI?
FANCY!
Thanks for being such a GREAT FRIEND, Chiby! Thank you ALL!
No problem.
We'd better go before we're LATE!
PSST- So you're still gonna paint and STUFF?
SURE I AM!
PHEW!
Come on!

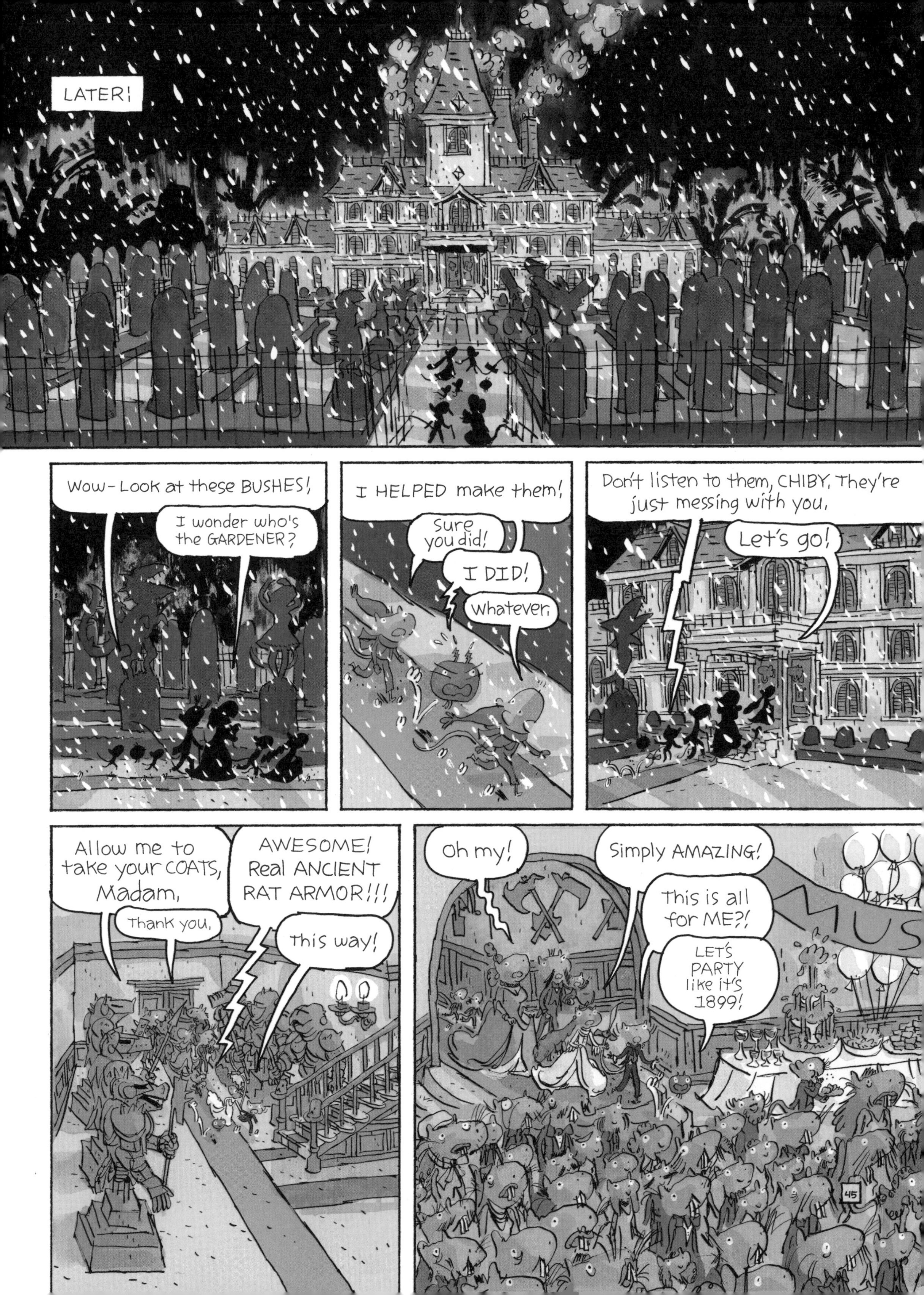
LATER:
Wow- Look at these BUSHES!
I wonder who's the GARDENER?
I HELPED make them!
Sure you did!
I DID!
Whatever.
Don't listen to them, CHIBY. They're just messing with you.
Let's go!
Allow me to take your COATS, Madam.
Thank you.
AWESOME! Real ANCIENT RAT ARMOR!!!
This way!
Oh my!
Simply AMAZING!
This is all for ME?!
LET'S PARTY like it's 1899!

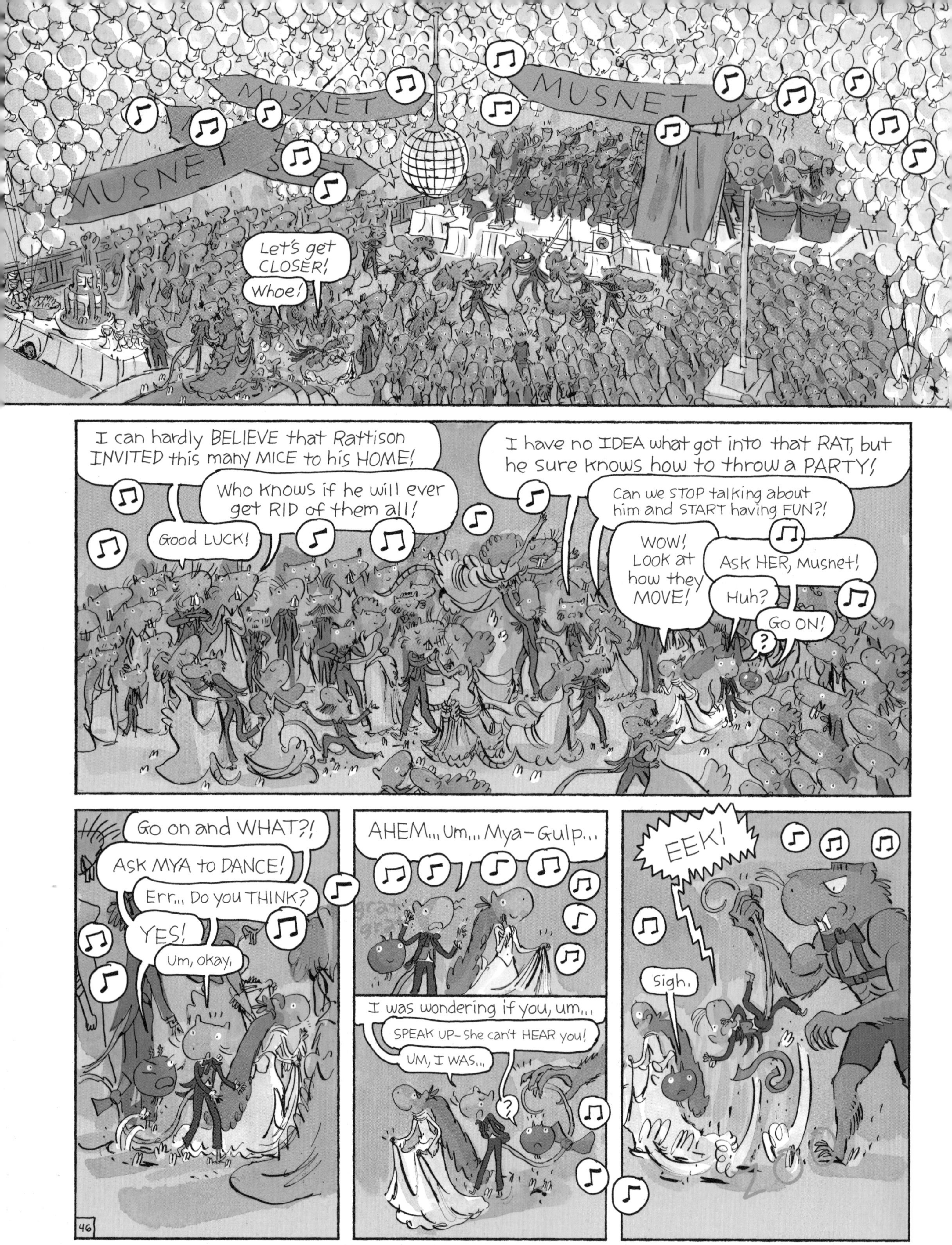
MUSNET
MUSNET
MUSNET
Let's get CLOSER!
Whoe!
I can hardly BELIEVE that Rattison INVITED this many MICE to his HOME!
Who knows if he will ever get RID of them all!
Good LUCK!
I have no IDEA what got into that RAT, but he sure knows how to throw a PARTY!
Can we STOP talking about him and START having FUN?!
WOW! LOOK at how they MOVE!
Ask HER, Musnet!
Huh?
Go ON!
?
Go on and WHAT?!
Ask MYA to DANCE!
Err... Do you THINK?
YES!
Um, okay.
AHEM... Um... Mya-Gulp...
I was wondering if you, um...
SPEAK UP- She can't HEAR you!
UM, I WAS...
?
EEK!
Sigh.

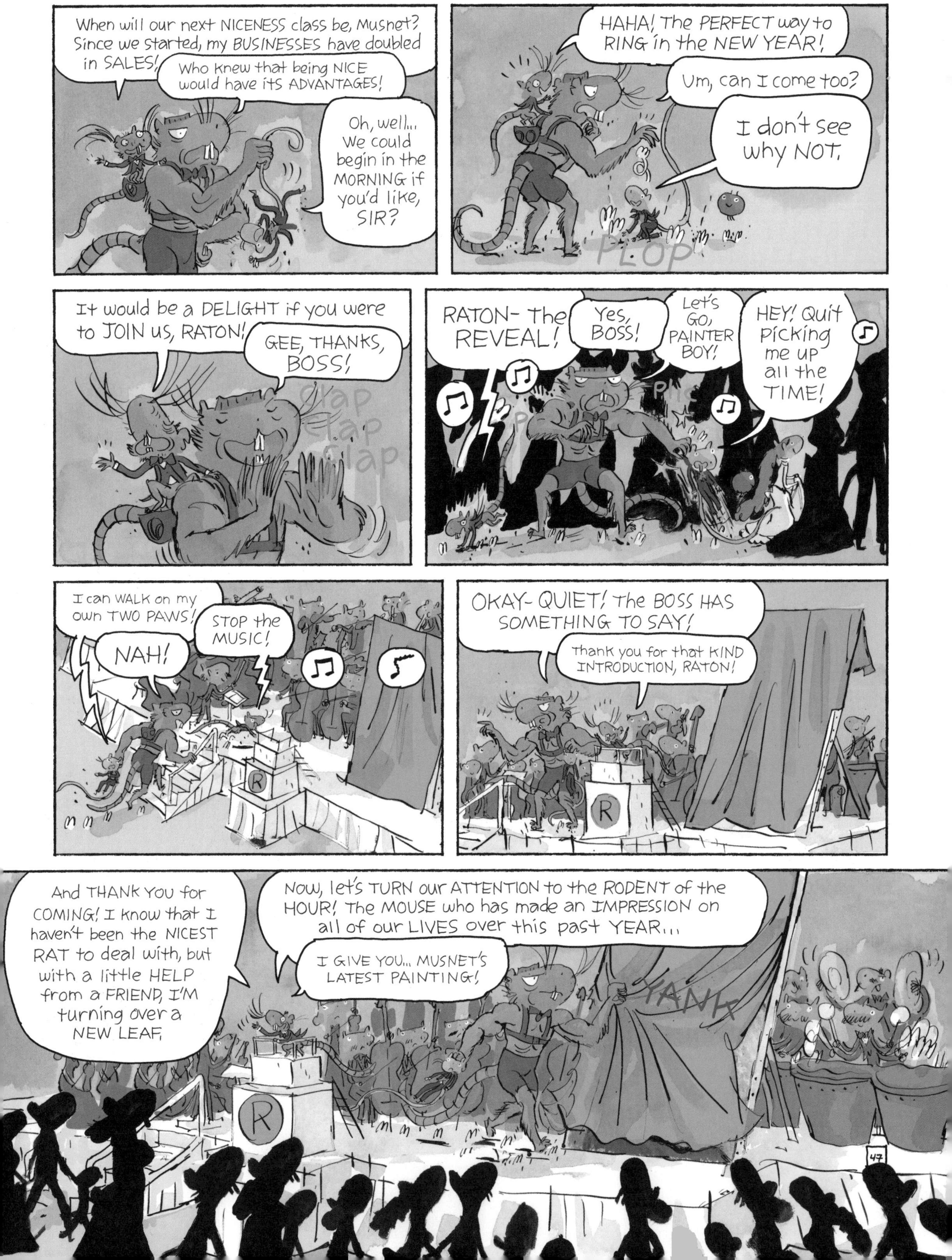
When will our next NICENESS class be, Musnet? Since we started, my BUSINESSES have doubled in SALES!
Who knew that being NICE would have its ADVANTAGES!
Oh, well... We could begin in the MORNING if you'd like, SIR?
HAHA! The PERFECT way to RING in the NEW YEAR!
Um, can I come too?
I don't see why NOT.
PLOP
It would be a DELIGHT if you were to JOIN us, RATON!
GEE, THANKS, BOSS!
clap clap clap
RATON- the REVEAL!
Yes, BOSS!
Let's GO, PAINTER BOY!
HEY! Quit picking me up all the TIME!
I can WALK on my own TWO PAWS!
NAH!
STOP the MUSIC!
OKAY- QUIET! The BOSS HAS SOMETHING TO SAY!
Thank you for that KIND INTRODUCTION, RATON!
And THANK YOU for COMING! I know that I haven't been the NICEST RAT to deal with, but with a little HELP from a FRIEND, I'M turning over a NEW LEAF.
Now, let's TURN our ATTENTION to the RODENT of the HOUR! The MOUSE who has made an IMPRESSION on all of our LIVES over this past YEAR...
I GIVE YOU... MUSNET'S LATEST PAINTING!
YANK
R

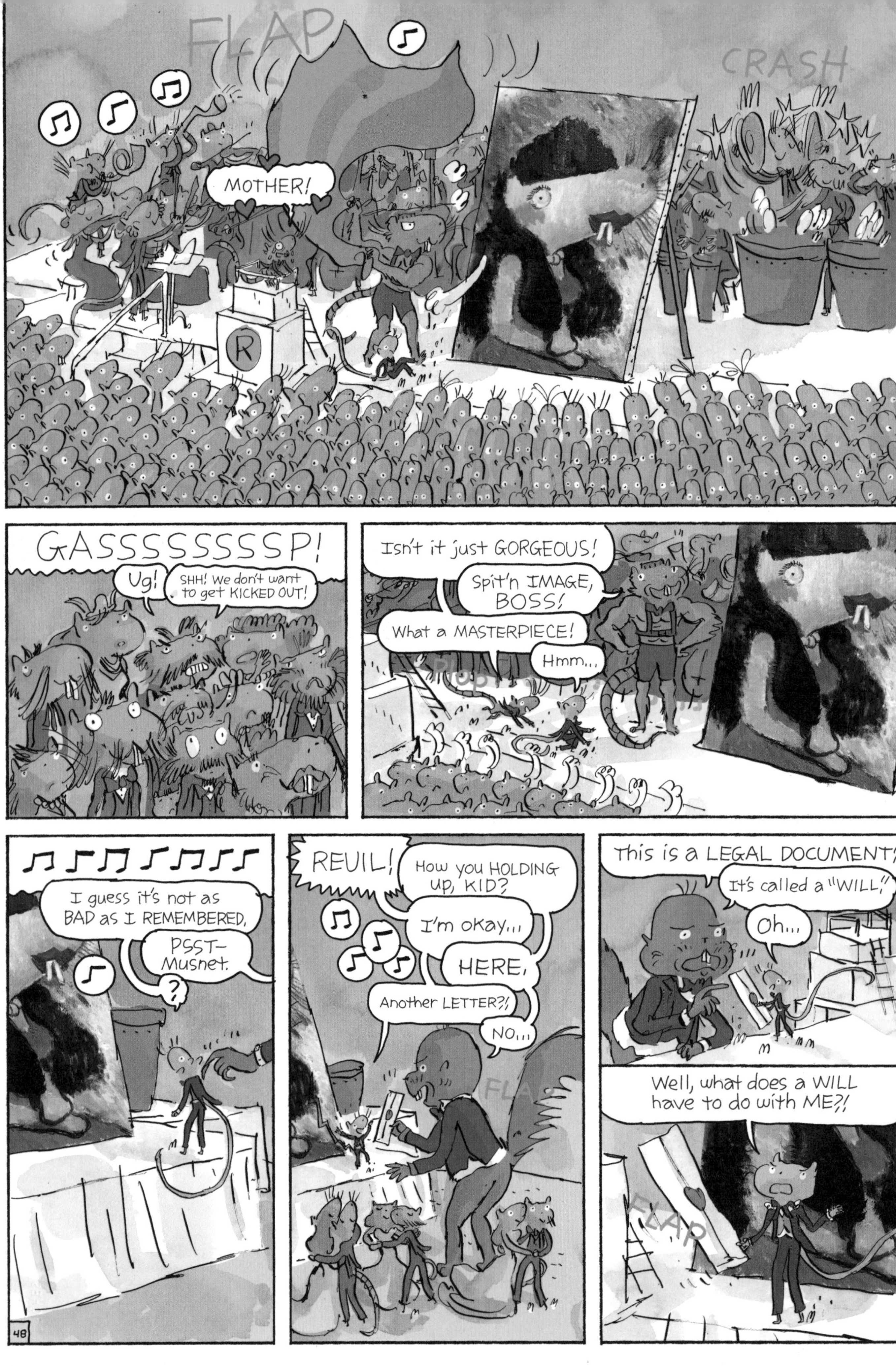

FLAP
CRASH
MOTHER!
R
GASSSSSSSSP!
Ug!
SHH! We don't want to get KICKED OUT!
Isn't it just GORGEOUS!
Spit'n IMAGE, BOSS!
What a MASTERPIECE!
Hmm...
I guess it's not as BAD as I REMEMBERED.
PSST- Musnet.
?
REUIL!
How you HOLDING UP, KID?
I'm okay...
HERE.
Another LETTER?!
NO...
FLA
This is a LEGAL DOCUMENT!
It's called a "WILL."
Oh...
Well, what does a WILL have to do with ME?!
FLAP

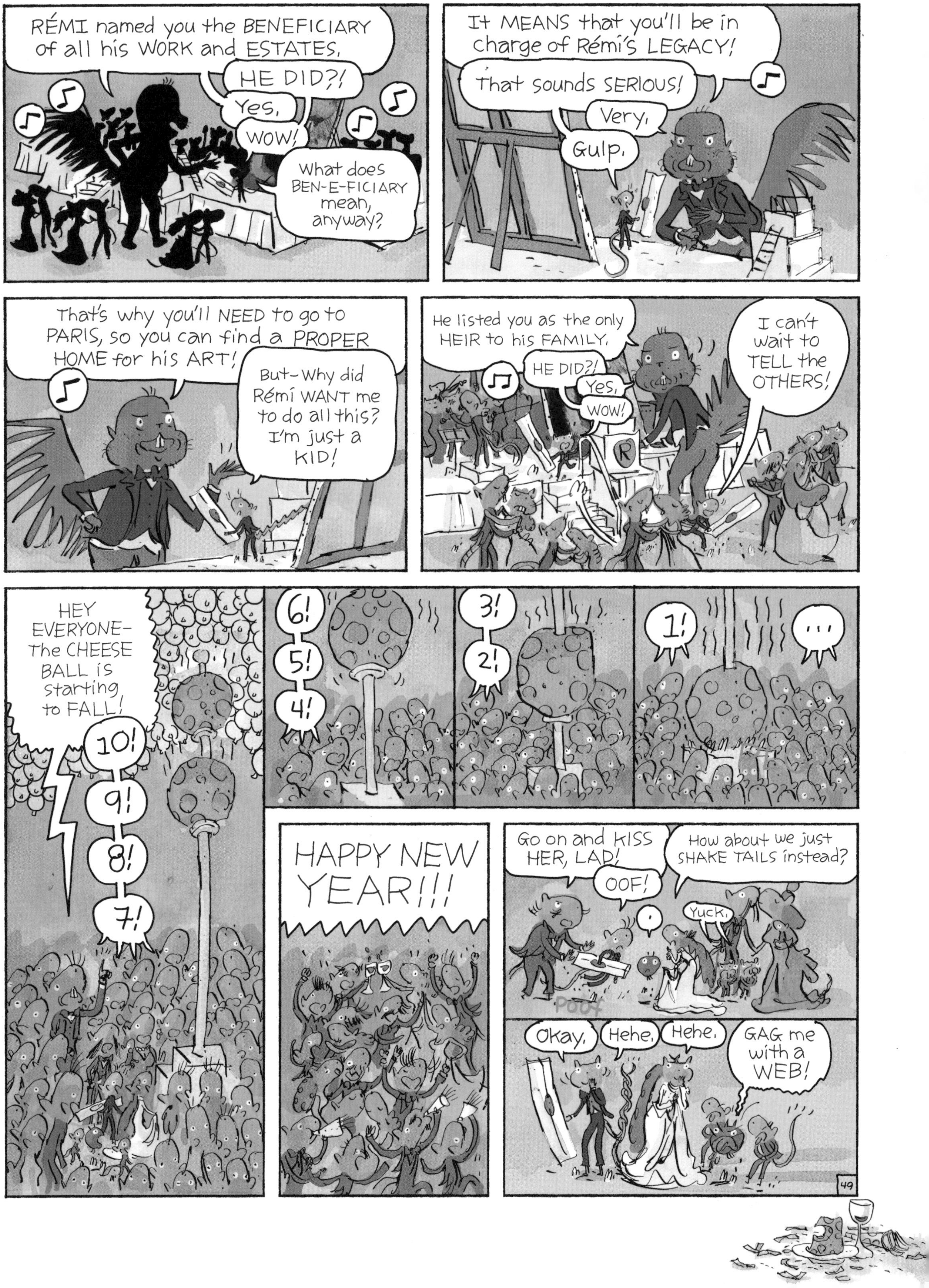
RÉMI named you the BENEFICIARY of all his WORK and ESTATES.
HE DID?!
Yes.
WOW!
What does BEN-E-FICIARY mean, anyway?
It MEANS that you'll be in charge of Rémi's LEGACY!
That sounds SERIOUS!
Very.
Gulp.
That's why you'll NEED to go to PARIS, so you can find a PROPER HOME for his ART!
But- Why did Rémi WANT me to do all this? I'm just a KID!
He listed you as the only HEIR to his FAMILY.
HE DID?!
Yes.
WOW!
I can't wait to TELL the OTHERS!
HEY EVERYONE- The CHEESE BALL is starting to FALL!
10!
9!
8!
7!
6!
5!
4!
3!
2!
1!
...
HAPPY NEW YEAR!!!
Go on and KISS HER, LAD!
OOF!
How about we just SHAKE TAILS instead?
Yuck.
POOF
Okay.
Hehe.
Hehe.
GAG me with a WEB!

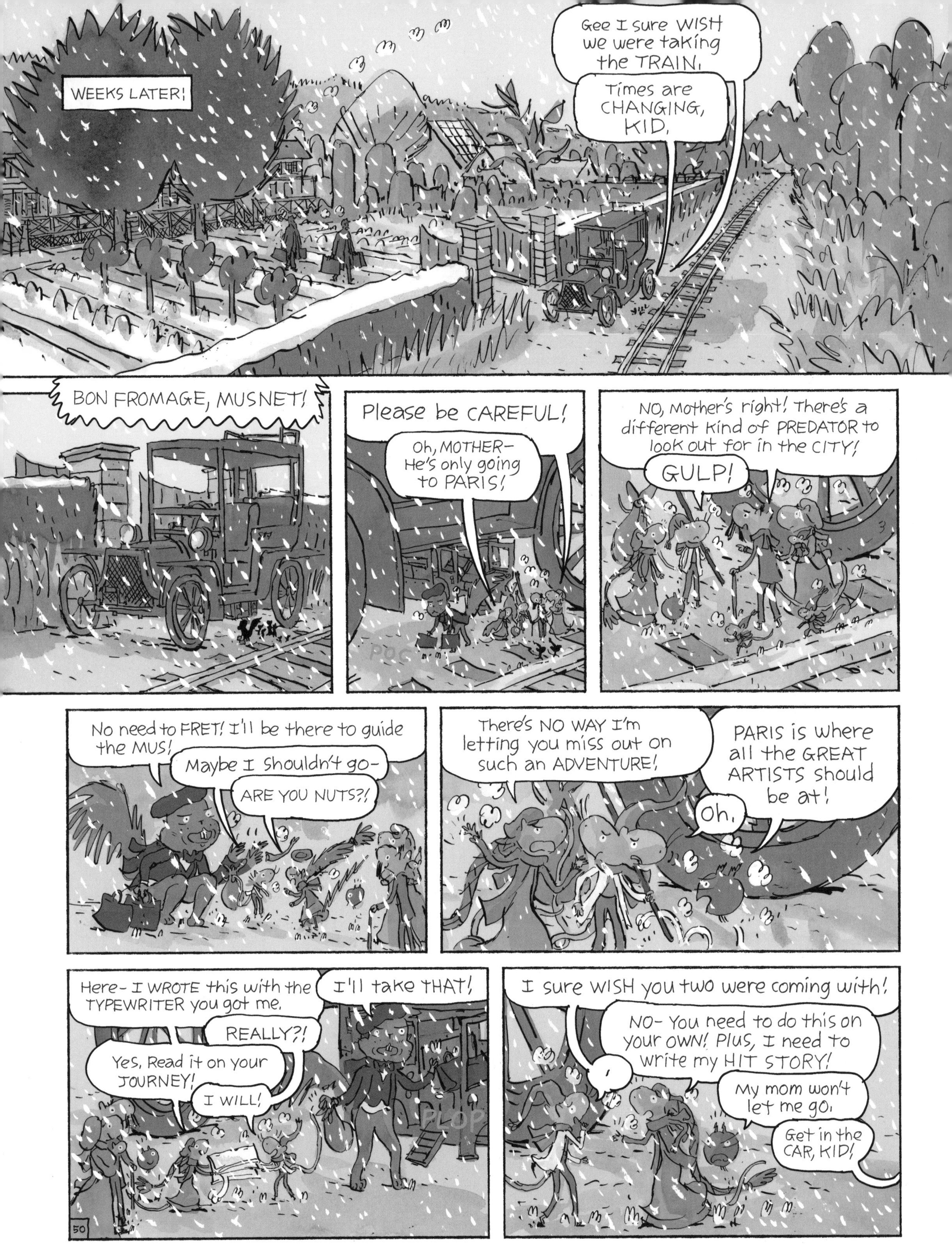

WEEKS LATER!
Gee I sure WISH we were taking the TRAIN.
Times are CHANGING, KID.
BON FROMAGE, MUSNET!
Please be CAREFUL!
Oh, MOTHER– He's only going to PARIS!
POC
NO, Mother's right! There's a different kind of PREDATOR to look out for in the CITY!
GULP!
No need to FRET! I'll be there to guide the MUS!
Maybe I shouldn't go–
ARE YOU NUTS?!
There's NO WAY I'm letting you miss out on such an ADVENTURE!
PARIS is where all the GREAT ARTISTS should be at!
Oh.
Here– I WROTE this with the TYPEWRITER you got me.
I'll take THAT!
REALLY?!
Yes. Read it on your JOURNEY!
I WILL!
PLOP
I sure WISH you two were coming with!
NO– You need to do this on your OWN! PLUS, I need to write my HIT STORY!
My mom won't let me go.
Get in the CAR, KID!

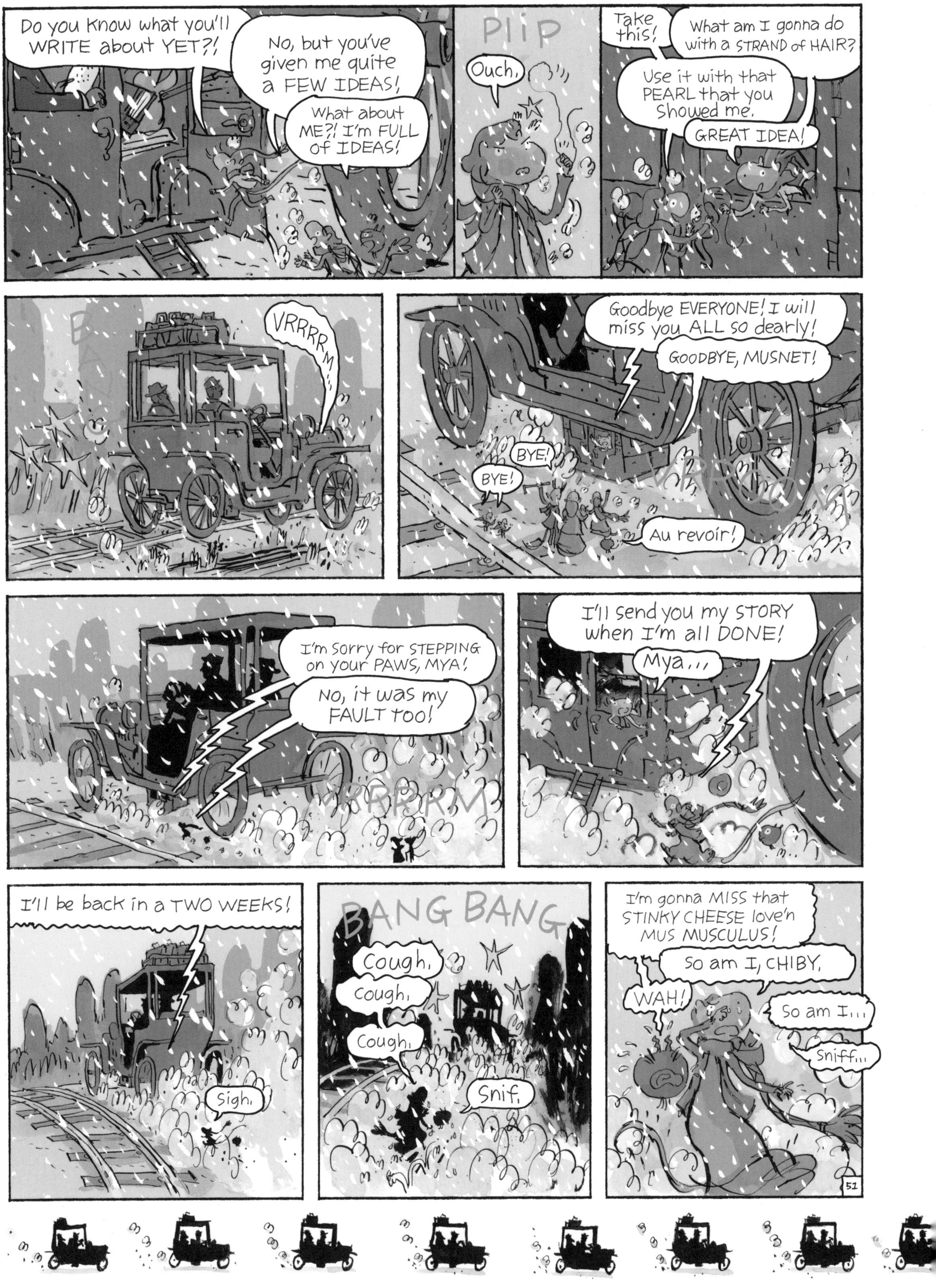

Do you know what you'll WRITE about YET?!
No, but you've given me quite a FEW IDEAS!
What about ME?! I'm FULL of IDEAS!
PLIP
Ouch!
Take this!
What am I gonna do with a STRAND of HAIR?
Use it with that PEARL that you showed me.
GREAT IDEA!
VRRRRRM
Goodbye EVERYONE! I will miss you ALL so dearly!
GOODBYE, MUSNET!
BYE!
BYE!
Au revoir!
I'm sorry for STEPPING on your PAWS, MYA!
No, it was my FAULT too!
VRRRRRM
I'll send you my STORY when I'm all DONE!
Mya...
I'll be back in a TWO WEEKS!
Sigh.
BANG BANG
Cough.
Cough.
Cough.
Snif.
I'm gonna MISS that STINKY CHEESE love'n MUS MUSCULUS!
So am I, CHIBY.
WAH!
So am I...
Sniff...

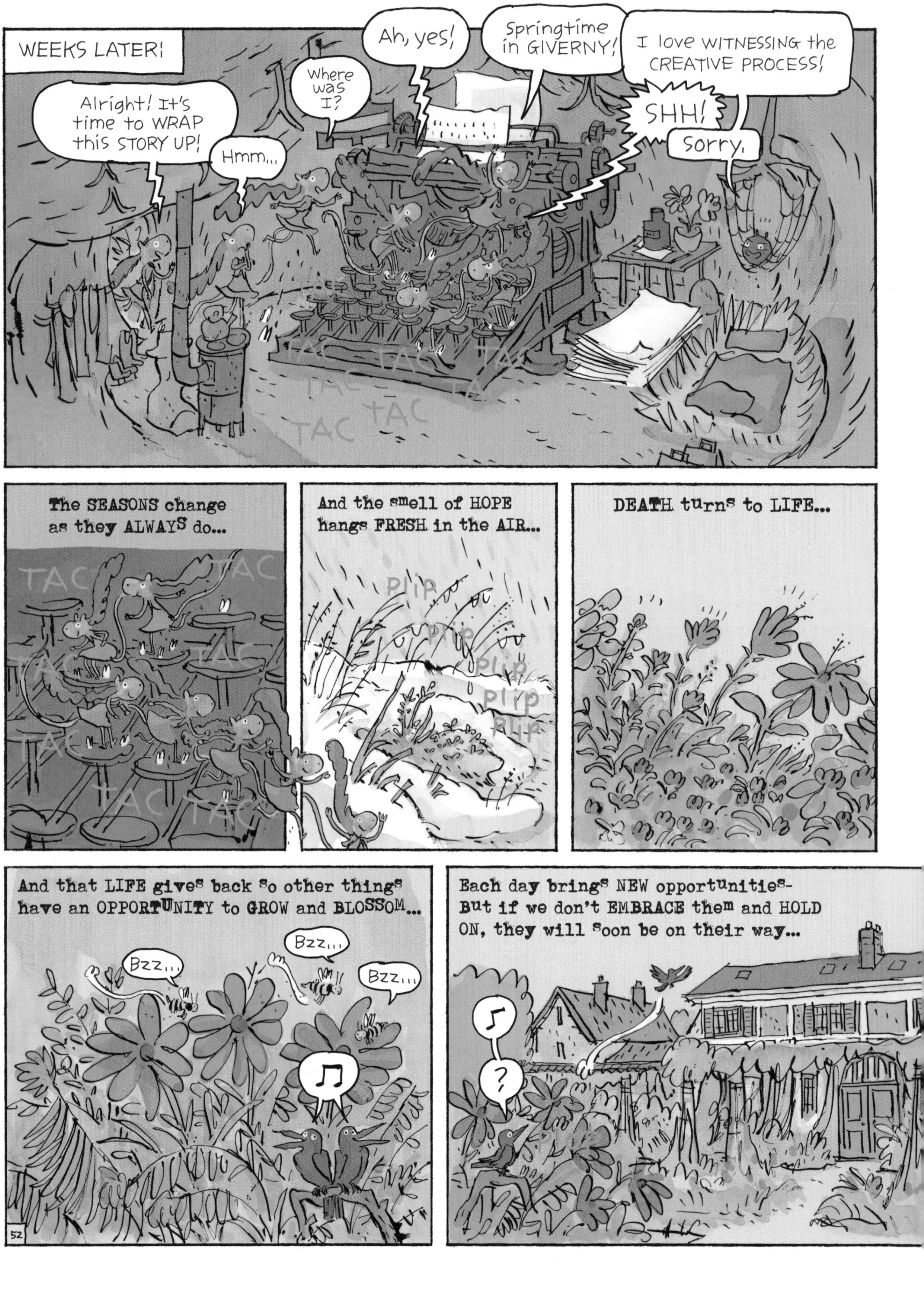

WEEKS LATER!
Alright! It's time to WRAP this STORY UP!
Hmm...
Where was I?
Ah, yes!
Springtime in GIVERNY!
I love WITNESSING the CREATIVE PROCESS!
SHH!
Sorry.
TAC TAC TAC TAC TAC TAC
The SEASONS change as they ALWAYS do...
TAC TAC TAC TAC TAC TAC
And the smell of HOPE hangs FRESH in the AIR...
Plip Plip Plip Plip Plip
DEATH turns to LIFE...
And that LIFE gives back so other things have an OPPORTUNITY to GROW and BLOSSOM...
Bzz...
Bzz...
Bzz...
♫
Each day brings NEW opportunities- But if we don't EMBRACE them and HOLD ON, they will soon be on their way...
♪
?

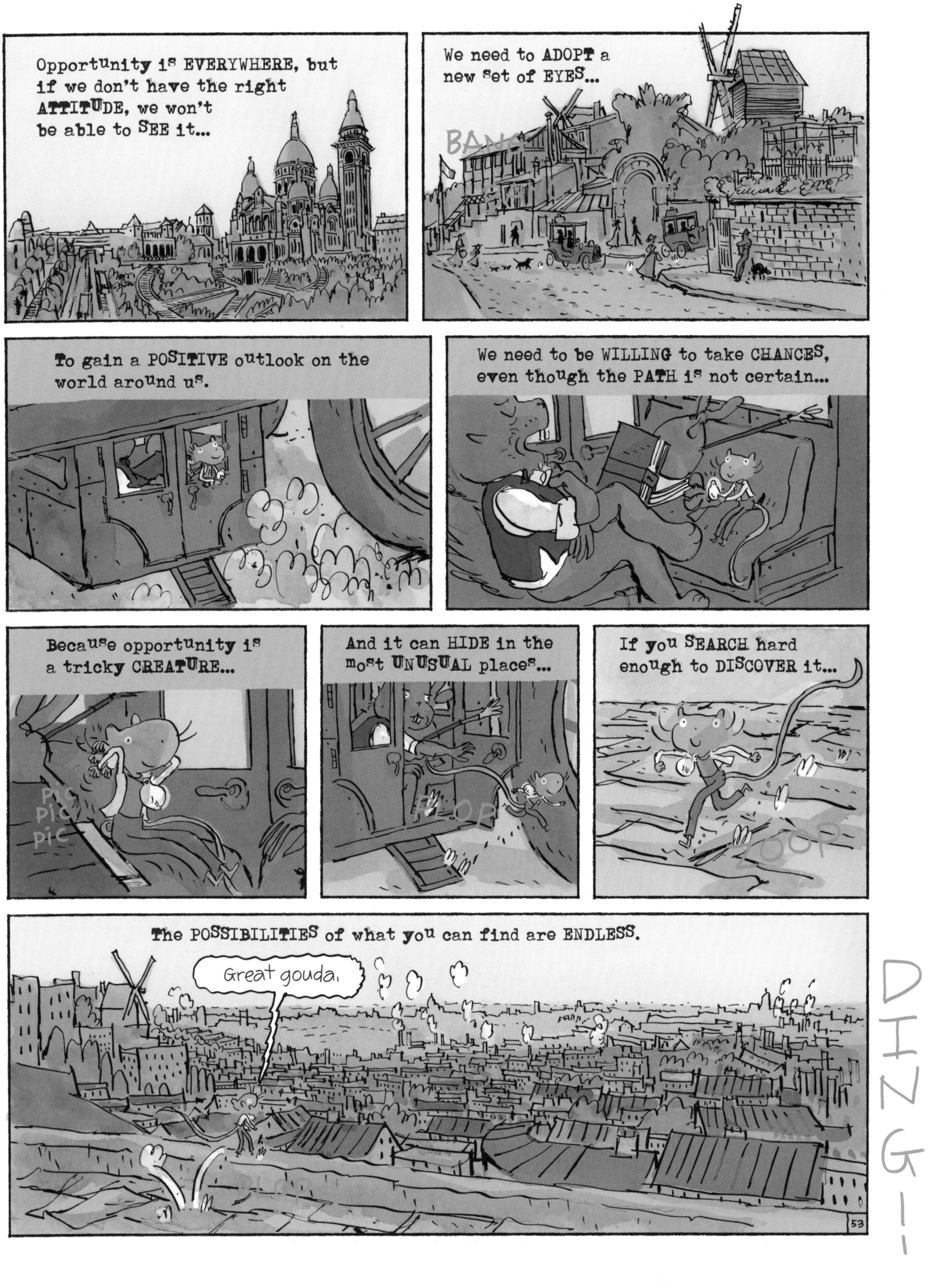
Opportunity is EVERYWHERE, but if we don't have the right ATTITUDE, we won't be able to SEE it...
We need to ADOPT a new set of EYES...
To gain a POSITIVE outlook on the world around us.
We need to be WILLING to take CHANCES, even though the PATH is not certain...
Because opportunity is a tricky CREATURE...
PIC PIC PIC
And it can HIDE in the most UNUSUAL places...
If you SEARCH hard enough to DISCOVER it...
ZOOP
The POSSIBILITIES of what you can find are ENDLESS.
Great gouda.
53
DING!!

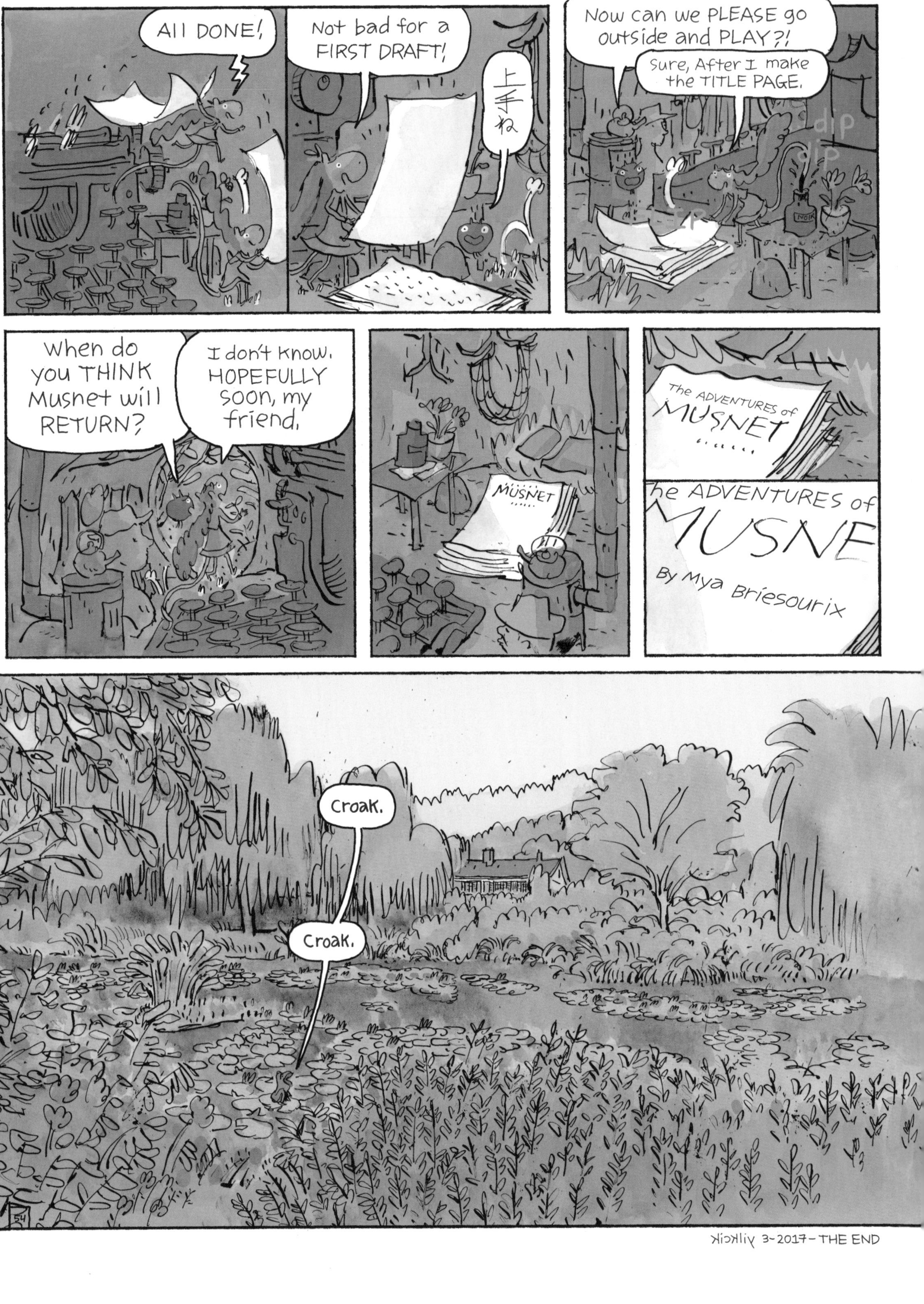
All DONE!
Not bad for a FIRST DRAFT!
上手ね
Now can we PLEASE go outside and PLAY?!
Sure, After I make the TITLE PAGE.
dip
dip
When do you THINK Musnet will RETURN?
I don't know. HOPEFULLY soon, my friend.
MUSNET
The ADVENTURES of MUSNET
he ADVENTURES of MUSNE
By Mya Briesourix
Croak.
Croak.

kickliy 3-2017 - THE END